# GONE TO THE DOGS

*Also by Mary Guterson*

**WE ARE ALL FINE HERE**

# GONE

# TO THE

# DOGS

MARY GUTERSON

St. Martin's Griffin New York

This is a work of fiction. All of the characters, organizations, and events portrayed in this novel are either products of the author's imagination or are used fictitiously.

 Printed in the United States of America. For information, address St. Martin's Press, 175 Fifth Avenue, New York, N.Y. 10010.

www.stmartins.com

Library of Congress Cataloging-in-Publication Data

Guterson, Mary.
Gone to the dogs / Mary Guterson.—1st ed.
p. cm.
ISBN-13: 978-0-312-54179-8
ISBN-10: 0-312-54179-1
1. Single women—Fiction. 2. Domestic fiction. I. Title.
PS3607.U79G66 2009
813'.6—dc22 2009010691

10 9 8 7 6 5 4 3 2

For Rob

# GONE TO THE DOGS

*I didn't actually steal the dog. I invited it over—him over—and he very kindly accepted my invitation. I don't think I can be blamed for the dog's interest in me and the contents of my car. He was bored to death out there in that little doggy pen they'd built for him. Sitting alone, waiting for action. Well, not exactly sitting, more like lying. Asleep. Until I came by and woke him up. But I'm sure he must have been very, very bored because otherwise would he have been sound asleep in the middle of the afternoon?*

*I opened my car door, and he jumped in like he owned the place. He didn't hesitate. He didn't even sniff around, only sat himself down on the front passenger seat, his big juicy tongue hanging out of his big juicy mouth. He looked very ready for action.*

*Now, I ask you. Is that stealing?*

*Okay, it's stealing.*

*Here's the thing: My boyfriend left me, so I took the dog. I know it sounds like a flimsy excuse. But it's not really all that flimsy when you consider the minor, inconsequential, not to mention apparently forgettable detail that we'd been engaged, Brian and me. "Engaged," as in "planning to be married." I guess you could say we had a massive breakdown in communication. Somehow, I'd been under the impression that when we decided to get married, that meant, you know, "matrimony." Ring, white dress, honeymoon in Hawaii, that sort of thing. While to my former fiancé, deciding to get married turned out to be code for "decamp immediately for the tall, blond, athletic thing's vagina."*

*Ha! I wasn't the love of his life! Sure, it would have been nice to learn this crucial piece of information a tad earlier—say, six or seven years earlier—but things don't always go the way we want them to, now, do they?*

*I looked at the tag on the dog's purple collar.*

*"Tilly," it said. Is there a worse name for a dog anywhere on the planet? Tilly? It was a boy dog, for crying out loud. Didn't they notice?*

*"You are no longer Tilly," I said. "And you no longer wear an ugly purple collar."*

*I don't know what gets into me sometimes. Five minutes before, I'd had no intentions of becoming a dog owner. Just goes to show, you never know what the future may bring.*

# 1

The first time I caught sight of the former Tilly was on a Sunday in early September, the same Sunday I'd been invited to brunch at my mother's. I wasn't looking forward to this particular Sunday brunch, and not only because my mother can't make toast, much less any of the brunchlike items one would normally expect to be served when invited to a meal scheduled for midday Sunday. No. It's that in all my life, I'd never heard my mother say the words *Sunday brunch* before. Sunday, yes. Brunch, she may have uttered once or twice in her fifty-eight years. But never the two words together. So I knew something was up.

My mother is the last of the great matchmakers. Show her an unattached human of any size, shape, age, or intellect, and her mind will start ticking immediately as she browses the mental files of other unattached humans she keeps stashed in her brain for her matchmaking purposes. Nothing makes her happier than to bring together two otherwise lost and lonely souls. No matter that the lost and lonely souls may be enjoying their lost and lonely status and have no want of a lifelong mate or even a date for Sunday brunch. Mother knows best. Odd souls need each other whether they want each other or not.

Especially odd daughter souls.

Sure enough, on that morning in September, I walked into her house to find a strange man in a beige sweater and metal-framed glasses sitting on her living room sofa, a man I did my best not to look at. His glasses were the oversize aviator kind, and he had a mustache and black hair combed neatly over his forehead. He looked exactly like a serial killer.

"Mother," I said.

She was in the kitchen, poking her finger at something pie-shaped, wrapped in layers of tinfoil, on the oven shelf.

"Not quite done," she said, slamming the oven door shut.

"Who is the serial killer in the living room?"

"I don't know what you're talking about."

If one sentence could sum up an entire mother/daughter relationship, my mother had just spoken it.

My mother didn't look like my mother. Usually, my mother dresses exactly like the ample-bodied, former hippie, current social worker that she is: drapey pants, tunic tops in earthy tones, woven scarves, a pair of flats. But today she'd traded in her normal attire for something else altogether—a knee-length navy skirt, a fitted white blouse unbuttoned enough to display a dramatic peek of maternal cleavage, and most surprising of all, a pair of leather boots that looked to be uncomfortably squeezing the tops of her calves. She resembled a schoolgirl, albeit one who had flunked a few dozen times. I didn't say a word—just because my mother never missed an opportunity to comment on my appearance didn't mean I had to stoop to her level. I only looked at her. Intensely. Had she lost her mind?

"What?" she said, as if she didn't know.

"Oh, nothing," I said.

I've learned from long experience that it's best to avoid all possible conflict-causing topics with my mother. Which probably explains why we never talk. How it is that my mother shows daily understanding for unwed teenage mothers while never managing to show an ounce of understanding for me is a conundrum I prefer not to analyze.

She pulled a big glass bowl of lettuce greens from the refrigerator and set it on the counter.

"Are your hands clean?" she asked me.

"I'm not interested in him."

"No one told you to be interested in anybody."

"Good. I'm glad that's clear."

"Toss the salad, would you?"

I said I would and she said to wash my hands first and I said thanks for reminding me, otherwise I might have forgotten. I sliced up a tomato and threw it over the lettuce.

"His name is Ronald," my mother said. "Be nice to him."

"I'm always nice."

"Ha!"

Right then my sister, Alicia, walked in wearing a new wig. One with long bangs and a little flip at the shoulders. Very sixties.

"Hi, Rena," she said to me. And then she winked.

"I know. Serial killer," I said.

"He's not that bad."

"You take him, then."

"I'm spoken for."

Which was the truth. Alicia, who calls herself Aviva, has been married to her eye doctor husband, Aryeh—formerly Alan—for nine years now. They have five kids. Five. And I don't believe they are finished repopulating the world. Fortunately, that morning she'd left all of those five kids at home with Aryeh.

"It's kosher, right?" Alicia asked, pointing at the oven. She gave my mother's schoolgirl getup a quick glance up and down but expertly refrained from either making a face or commenting. Instead she only threw me a questioning look, to which I replied with a shrug of my shoulders. We've had similar nonverbal conversations for as long as I can remember. We may be four years apart in age (Alicia is the older one), not to mention worlds apart in lifestyle, but we share a mother, and that's more than enough to permanently connect us.

"Of course it's kosher," our mother said. "You think I'd feed you something that wasn't kosher?"

"Where did you buy it?"

After that, I stopped listening. I can't stand all the kosher/

nonkosher talk. Two more minutes and Alicia was going to say a little prayer at the sink and pour water over her hands from a special water pitcher. The whole thing makes me nuts. One day, I will come to grips with my sister's conversion from secular bagel-and-cream-cheese-we-don't-believe-in-Jesus-but-I'm-not-sure-what-it-is-we-do-believe-in Jew to Orthodox-wig-wearing mother of five. But that day seems awfully far in the future.

I concentrated instead on the ceramic dancing Mexicans that had landed on the ledge over my mother's sink since the last time I'd visited. My mother's house has long been stuffed to the gills with artsy tchotchkes from various worldly outposts. Growing up, I always wished we could have a normal house, the kind with a single painting on a wall or a coffee table with nothing on its surface, instead of a place that looked like an importer's emporium. But by now I'd gotten used to my mother's organized chaos. In fact, I hate to admit it, but in that moment, I sort of coveted the dancing Mexicans.

I was shaking a bottle of Italian dressing I'd found in the fridge when suddenly I felt my mother's fingertips in my hair.

"What are you *doing*?" I said.

"There's a piece sticking out," she said.

"God," I said.

I looked at my sister.

"I mean, *Gosh*."

Alicia ignored me.

My hair has been a constant source of exasperation to my mother since the day I popped out of her womb, famously hirsute. The way I see it, if she hadn't wanted a daughter with a head of massive, out-of-control curls, she very well could have married into a different gene pool from my frizzy-haired father's. She made one more pass at my head with what I now noticed were French-manicured fingernails. What, had she won a makeover at a synagogue raffle?

"Enough!" I said.

I poured the dressing over the salad.

"Go out and talk to Ronald," my mother said to me. "Go on."

"I don't want to talk to Ronald," I said.

"Don't be rude. He's our guest. Go offer him something to drink. You can do it. I know you can."

It did seem awfully impolite to be avoiding the serial killer on the living room sofa any longer. What if he got angry at being left alone and decided to add the three of us to the dozens of bodies he already had stashed in his basement freezer?

I went into the living room.

"You must be Ronald," I said. "Can I get you something to drink?"

Ronald looked at me. I think. His glasses were awfully thick.

"Call me Ron," he said. "And no, thank you."

He kept looking at me. I was stuck. If only he'd given me a drink order, I'd have something purposeful to do. But there was no drink order. There was nothing. Just Ron, looking in my direction. His mustache was the kind that hangs over the top lip like a little furry curtain. I sat on the edge of the overstuffed club chair across from the sofa. From the kitchen came the sound of my mother banging shut the oven door again.

"Five more minutes!" she called out.

"So, Ron," I said. "What is it you do?"

It's exactly the kind of question I hate to be asked, but I couldn't think of anything else. You've no idea how difficult it is to make conversation with a serial killer. I tried to look comfortable perched on the edge of the overstuffed club chair. The living room drapes had been pulled shut, as usual—my mother believes that the minute she opens the drapes she is inviting all of the neighbors in to know her business—leaving us in semidarkness. In this light, or lack of it, Ron looked shadowy and mysterious, which is a nice way of saying he looked awfully scary. In fact, he seemed to pretty well blend in with the collection of menacing tribal masks dotting the wall above his head.

"I'm a doctor," he said.

"A doctor. What kind of doctor?"

"A dermatologist."

"Uh-huh," I said. "Great. You must get a lot of people asking you to look at their moles at parties."

"Not really."

I nodded. I tried not to think about Ron looking at people's moles or whatever else he must look at day after day in his office. It seemed to me that being a dermatologist is probably the grossest of all professions. You're just asking people to show up and reveal the disgusting whatever-it-is they've got growing on their body. I couldn't imagine who would want Ron looking at their disgusting whatever-it-is, although come to think of it, having a dermatologist who isn't all that good-looking is probably preferable to showing your body to a sweet young handsome doctor.

Ron raised his eyebrows and tilted his head toward me.

"Do you have a mole you're concerned about?" he asked.

"Oh, no!" I said. "No, no, no."

Then I laughed very hard to show how funny that was. Ron smiled. His mustache was now a straight line in the middle of his face.

"And you?" he asked me. "What is it that you do?"

"Good question," I said.

It wasn't a good question. It was a horrible question. Because there was no way to disguise the answer into something even remotely respectable. I was a waitress. No matter that I was a very good waitress. No matter that being a very good waitress entails honing a set of skills that would leave most people dangling at the end of their rope: physical stamina, a firm memory, attention to detail, not to mention the ability to deal with total assholes on a daily basis without resorting to violence. And yet each time I had to 'fess up to my chosen career—which I hadn't so much chosen as simply fallen into by circumstance—I felt as though I were admitting to failure. Who intends to be a waitress?

"I'm a waitress."

"That's nice."

"It's all right. It pays the bills."

"Good to get the bills paid."

"Yes. Yes, it is."

Ron nodded and I nodded back at him. We were both still nodding when my mother and Alicia finally came into the living room to join us. My mother's lips were newly painted with a shiny orange lipstick. Her hair fell past her shoulders in one enviously smooth wave. She smiled her huge smile. Ron stood up.

"I see the two of you have met," my mother said.

"Yes, we have," Ron said. He looked at me. "I mean, you must be Rena, right?"

My mother gave me her big-eye look, which is her way of demonstrating shock and disgust at the same time.

"Rena, you didn't tell him your name?"

"Rena," I said.

"Nice to meet you, Rena," Ron said.

"And this is my other daughter, Aviva," my mother said.

"Nice to meet you, Aviva."

"Well, now. Everybody hungry?" my mother asked. She smiled her huge smile again, which is her way of showing everyone how happy she is.

"I'm hungry," Ron said.

At that, my mother did a funny thing. She leaned toward Ron. She set her hand on his head and mussed his hair a little bit.

"Oh, I know *you're* hungry," she said to him.

It's not a very nice feeling to find out that the serial killer sitting in your mother's living room is not, in fact, the blind date your mother has planned for you, but is instead your mother's date. The moment my mother mussed Dr. Ron's thick hair with her fifty-eight-year-old French-manicured fingers was the same moment I felt more sorry for myself than I had in ages. Suddenly the serial killer looked—dare I say it?—dangerously attractive. And very employed. He looked like a guy with potential, with features you might be able to work with. The mustache, for example. It could be shaved, couldn't it? And the aviator glasses? I suddenly imagined Ron in a pair of tiny black frames. European style. Just sweep that hair off his forehead, and voilà! But, no. There would be no Ron improvement sessions. At least not taught by me.

Somehow we got through brunch. Ron turned out to be an all right guy. He was very polite and also a neat eater, which is always a plus. He was adept at wiping his mustache clean of bits of food. He seemed genuinely interested in the mishmash of topics my mother brought up. She, in turn, laughed at everything he said. It was sickening.

Okay, I told myself, time to take the high road. I will not be a baby about my mother's decision to discard her former life—one that seriously lacked in the romance department—and begin a new one. After all, there's nothing wrong with a little change every now and then, a little forward momentum. No need to feel selfishly envious of the fact that my mother had gone and found herself a nice serial killer to love. In fact, I hoped they'd be very happy together. My mother certainly looked happy enough. I decided she was my new role model. She'd spent twenty-nine years with my dad before the big split, and now look at her! Carrying on like a teenager!

I drove home from my mother's trying my best not to cry, but the radio stations had it in for me, playing one lovesick ballad after another. By the time I remembered that I had the power to turn off the radio, I was a basket case. What I needed at that moment was a big bag of chemically flavored microwave popcorn, a glass of red wine, and the three DVDs awaiting me back at my apartment in celebration of John Cusack Weekend. This was my third John Cusack Weekend in a row, but I was kind of stuck on Lloyd Dobler at the moment, and since there was no longer anyone to stop me from watching whatever the hell I pleased—suggesting we have yet another James Bond Weekend, for instance, or that one time when it was Sylvester Stallone Weekend, of all things—I went ahead and gave John Cusack a third weekend of his own.

I had no intentions at that moment of driving past Brian's new house, the one where he now lived with the tall, blond, athletic thing who had taken my place. In fact, I was as surprised as anyone to find myself turning slowly onto Cascade Boulevard. And yet there I was, cruising up the street, hoping

I wouldn't be caught by the happy couple, my eyes scanning the block for evidence of anything Brian-like. Two-thirds of the way up the block, I saw his dirty blue Honda. And a moment later, there *she* was, tall, blond, and athletic, prancing about on the front lawn of their charming white bungalow with a dog the size of a Volkswagen. So that's what she looked like. Long legs, long blond hair, a waist the width of a ten-year-old's. Perfect, it's called.

I was so busy looking at my replacement that for a moment I didn't give much attention to the dog. But then it suddenly came to me: They'd gotten a dog. Together. The two of them. I realize it's not exactly the same thing as having a baby, but still. Brian and I had never come *close* to getting a pet together. We didn't even have an apartment together. We had my apartment and we had Brian's apartment and we stayed most nights at my apartment because between the two of us, I changed the sheets more often.

A goddamned dog.

I waited an hour before driving by again, and then once more before work. That evening, I served burgers and steaks and fish platters to hungry restaurant patrons and hoped for some decent tips. I thought the same thoughts I'd been thinking for three months. If only I had a gun, I thought. Or, if only I had the guts to whack off his penis and toss it out the car window. Or—a new one to add to my list—I wonder how the tall, blond, athletic thing would look in a wheelchair. Things like that.

I made lousy tips.

Lisa, who worked my same shift, suggested I stop swearing at the customers.

I decided to become athletic, changed my mind, decided to become athletic, changed my mind, decided to become athletic, changed my mind, decided to become athletic, got drunk.

All in all, it wasn't a very good day.

# 2

Before the big breakup, we'd been together for seven years, Brian and me. Seven. Years. Three-fourths of a decade. One-quarter of my life, practically. My youthful prime. Sure, we'd had one or two momentary tragic breakups and delirious reunions. What couple doesn't go through a few ups and downs? But through it all I had remained hopelessly smitten, thoroughly certain we would always be Brian and Rena, growing old together. I had pictured it all already. Pictured the beautiful babies we would have together—little miniatures of Brian in boy and girl versions. Pictured the pictures of the beautiful babies we'd have together organized in a nice photo album next to all of the other albums of photos, which we would keep on a shelf in our family room in the house we would buy together after photo-filled trips to Europe and the Caribbean. I had pictured that same house invaded by grandchildren—grandchildren! Had imagined

Brian old and toothless, and the sweet way I would mash his food for him and then spoon it into his old, toothless mouth.

But none of it was to be.

Here's more or less what happened:

Brian, who is the athletic sort, took off to kayak through the Grand Canyon. He was supposed to be gone for two weeks. And when he came back, we were going to tell the world of our engagement plans. I waited patiently. I drew ideas for our wedding invitations on big pads of paper. I compared prices on sit-down dinners for three hundred. I considered a big tent with a barbecue and a country western band. Or maybe we'd go the humble pot-luck route—I'd leave my feet bare and wear flowers in my hair. I tried on a few dozen wedding dresses. I made charts of how long it would take me to lose twenty pounds. I decided I didn't need to lose twenty pounds, I only needed to lose ten. I compromised at fifteen.

The two weeks ended. The phone didn't ring. I waited patiently. Maybe his plane had been delayed. Maybe there hadn't been enough water in the river and the trip had taken much longer than planned. Maybe Brian had been so distracted by shopping in Colorado for my engagement ring that he'd lost all track of time.

I wasn't worried yet. Over the course of our years together, Brian had extended or cut short plenty of trips with little or no notice. It wouldn't be at all unusual for a two-week outing of his to turn into three. An expedition he once took to Alaska lasted an extra ten days. Of course, he was lost that time and the forest service had to send out a search party to find him. But that's not the point.

I thought of the fight we'd had before he left on his trip. Was that the reason I hadn't heard from him? Was he still mad at me because I'd been mad at the way he'd managed for the fourth year in a row to be conveniently out of town during the date of the annual Sammy's Place employee summer barbecue? I suppose I had made a pretty big deal of it. But that's what happens when your boyfriend makes a promise and then breaks it, right? A person has a right to get angry, doesn't she?

"Look," he'd said to me in that tone he used whenever he was frustrated at my inability to see the obvious—the obvious being his side of things. "I'm actually relieved I'll be missing it. I mean, *you* like the people you work with. But to *me* . . ."

"To you, what?"

"Come on. You know what I think of your buddies at the restaurant."

"Refresh my memory," I said.

Brian didn't hesitate.

"All right," he said. "They're losers, Rena. Come on. You know that."

God, I hated to admit it, but a small part of me—the part of me that made me feel small, not to mention disgusted with myself—*did* know that. Of course, I'd never use the word *loser.* Still, none of us who'd stuck around serving platters at

Sammy's Place year after year had meant to stay on after our first few months. It wasn't that we were lazy—if anything, just the opposite—it was more that we lacked the crucial ingredient necessary to cook up a proper future. Drive, you might call it. Or ambition. Or, in my case, knowing what I wanted my future to look like in the first place.

But I wasn't going to say any of that to Brian. I wasn't prepared to actually verbalize my own failings, despite the fact that my boyfriend was well acquainted with all of them. Besides, I worked with some very nice people. Very nice people with little drive or ambition, perhaps, but very nice people nevertheless. Okay, we were losers. Was that so terrible?

By then, my heart was beating loud enough to wake a baby.

"You don't even know them!" I said. "You've never spent more than five minutes talking to any of them! And who do you think you are, anyway? Not everybody on the planet has to be a college graduate."

"You are."

"That's not the point."

"Then what is the point?"

"The point is this makes four years in a row!"

"The point is, I got a permit to kayak the Grand Canyon! God, Rena. Think about it for a second, would you? Do you have any idea how hard it is to get a permit for the Grand Canyon? It can take years!"

"Four years in a row, Brian! God!"

"Quit that stupid job and I won't have to make it five!"

And on and on, until both of us were exhausted by the subject. Which was pretty much par for the course with Brian and me. We fought all of the time. And then we'd make up. And then we'd fight again. It was what we did. We were one of those dramatic couples that less dramatic couples are secretly envious of. All of that passion, twenty-four seven. No, it wasn't the fight that was keeping him from calling me.

Maybe Brian was only getting cold feet over our engagement. Suddenly, that seemed the most plausible explanation. Fear of the old ball and chain. Oh, Brian! Grow up!

A few more days went by.

I couldn't take it anymore. I called his parents.

"Say, Brian's not dead or anything, is he?" I said to Brian's dad when he picked up the phone.

"No, no, no," Mr. Benning said.

I could picture Brian's dad squeezing his watery gray eyes. Mr. Benning loved me. In fact, it often seemed possible that he loved me more than Brian did. During visits, he was always taking photographs of me, photographs that would later pop up in the Benning family photograph albums. He never failed to remember my birthday, year after year sending me a card in the mail along with a gift certificate to a bookstore or Nordstrom. When he and Mrs. Benning took their yearly trips to Arizona, he always brought me back something—a bracelet or necklace he'd come across that made him think of yours truly.

"Oh, the two of you will make such beautiful children together," he used to say.

Sometimes, I got the creepy feeling Mr. Benning was imagining the beautiful children he and I would make together, if only he could get Brian out of the picture. Not to mention the very slender and nervous Mrs. Benning. Although, come to think of it, maybe she was nervous only around me.

"What is it?" I asked now.

"Oh, Rena."

"What? What happened?"

Mr. Benning's voice took on a soft tone. "It seems our Boomer met someone in the Grand Canyon."

That's what they called Brian around the home front. Boomer.

"Met someone?"

I could hear Mr. Benning take a deep breath.

"Yes, dear," he said.

"Could you give me just a little more detail, Mr. Benning?"

"He met another girl, Rena. I'm sorry."

"Met another girl?"

"I'm really sorry, hon."

"He met another girl? What do you mean, he met another girl? You mean he has a new girlfriend?"

Mr. Benning took another deep breath before answering.

"He has a new girlfriend. Yes. He does."

"No."

"I'm afraid so."

"But we're supposed to get married! We're engaged!"

Mr. Benning coughed right into the receiver.

"Well, dear," he said after a moment. "All I know is that he met a new girl and her name is Anna and she's actually in the next room right now, watching television with Boomer. And I'm sorry that you didn't know."

I looked around the apartment. Brian's fleece jacket was hanging on a hook by the door. If I brought that jacket to my nose, it would smell exactly like him.

"Do you think you could go and get Boomer and put him on the phone?"

"Get him? You mean now?"

"Mr. Benning, please. Just put him on the phone."

I heard some muffled banging and a few loud voices, and finally Brian picked up another line.

"I got it, Dad!" he yelled.

"Okay! Well, good-bye, Rena," Mr. Benning said. "And I wish you the best of luck in everything."

"Got it, Dad," Brian said.

"Okay, then. Bye-bye, Rena."

"Good-bye, Mr. Benning."

"You take care, now."

"Dad!"

I heard the click of the telephone line as Mr. Benning hung up.

"Brian?"

"Hey."

"What's going on?"

"Yeah. Well. I'm glad you called. I was going to call you."

I waited, but he didn't say anything else.

"What's going on, Brian?"

"Yeah, well. You see. Yeah. I guess you heard."

"I want to hear it from you."

"I met someone else and we're moving in together."

"I can't believe this is happening."

"I'm sorry, Rena. I really am."

After that, there wasn't much else to say. I told Brian he was an asshole. And he said, Rena, please. And I said, Don't you Rena please me. And he said, Rena, please. And I said, You are such a fucking asshole. And he said, Rena, please. And so on. But really, the conversation had ended long before.

The last week of June seemed to last forever. I spent an hour or two boxing up the various items Brian had dumped at my apartment over the years and then spent the next couple of days staring at the boxes in the middle of the room. I kept picturing Brian showing up, out of breath, begging me to take him back.

Too late, buddy!

I thought of the way I would point at the boxes of his things I'd packed, declaring that he'd better get them out of the apartment—pronto!—or I'd be forced to take everything to the dump. Of course, I wouldn't mean it. I'd make him suffer for a few days, call him names, make him sleep on the edge of the bed without touching me. And then, I'd take him back.

I didn't hear from him. The closest I got to a message

from Brian was a note from Mr. Benning that arrived in the mail a week after our last phone conversation. I swear he'd sprayed that little white note with his musky cologne.

"Rena," it said. He'd written the "R" in "Rena" with a calligraphy pen, and it was very large and ornate. "Just to say how terribly saddened I am over recent events. Please know that you will be in our hearts forever. Yours, Thomas."

Apparently, the apple had, for once, fallen very far from the tree, because Brian himself didn't send a note, much less show up at my apartment, and after a few more days I really did take everything to the dump, cologne-scented note from his dad included. There wasn't all that much, actually. It just seemed like it. I stood over the big cargo bins, turned over the boxes, and watched Brian's things land in a pile on top of the rest of the garbage. There was his belt, lying in a snake-like coil over the sky blue bowling shirt I'd overpaid for at a vintage shop in San Francisco. There were his old Converse sneakers, his green fleece jacket, the sweater with a big star on the front his mom had knit for him the last Christmas that he'd immediately stashed in the back of my closet. A few books, a couple of T-shirts, the most recent issue of *Outside* magazine, a climbing rope. His toothbrush. I looked at all of it and, for just a moment, considered a dramatic jump into the bin myself, the way my grandfather had famously thrown himself on top of my grandmother's coffin after they'd put her in the hole in the ground. But unlike my grandfather, there'd be no soothing relatives to pull me free of Brian's garbage. There'd be only the bald guy in the wheelchair who took your entrance fee at the little booth at the front of the dump. So I didn't jump.

It was nearly August before Brian finally dashed off an e-mail, one where he managed to apologize without apologizing.

"I'm really sorry things ended so poorly," he wrote.

I tried, I honestly did, to come up with a rational, mature response but finally decided his nonapology apology didn't deserve one.

"You already left me," I wrote back. "Now leave me the fuck alone."

And wouldn't you know, good old Brian did exactly what I asked of him.

# 3

Honestly, I didn't lie awake at night dreaming of stealing the dog, a move that would surely break the tall, blond, athletic thing's heart, leading her inexorably into a depressive state that would, in turn, lead to the subsequent breakup of her relationship with my old boyfriend, after which he'd realize the errors of his ways and return to yours truly, tail between legs, begging for mercy. Although that wasn't a bad plan. No, I was fully prepared to get on with my life, or what was left to me of my life now that Brian had pretty much taken all of my dreams and crushed them into a very fine powder. But then, Derrick dropped by.

Of all of Brian's friends, I've always liked Derrick the most. Derrick and Brian have known each other since the third grade. They know each other better than anybody. So when he showed up to see how I was doing (it wasn't all that difficult for him, really—he lived on the second floor of my apartment building; I was on the third), I appreciated the effort, despite the ulterior motive behind it. Ever since I made the mistake of nearly, but not quite, sleeping with him three or four years ago (brief breakup, drunken stupor), Derrick has hovered in my background, waiting for another chance to possibly get in my pants. Stupidly, I find this behavior on his part flattering, even though I know Derrick's vaginal entry club has a nonexclusive policy.

"I don't know," I said. "Terrible, I guess. God. I mean, I just don't get what happened. What am I, an idiot? Was I supposed to see this coming?"

We were both sitting on my sofa, looking out the window at the street below. There wasn't anything to see but the occasional car driving by, the rain coming down, and every so often a student in a raincoat walking along the sidewalk. I still lived in the same apartment I'd had since grad school, and the neighborhood was mostly college students and former college students (like me and Derrick) who'd never managed to move away. My dirty laundry, which I'd cleared from the sofa to make room for the two of us, sat in a heap on the floor, tangled up with the clean laundry I'd dumped on the floor a few days earlier. For the next week or two, I'd have to use the sniff test to determine where my clothes fell in the laundry cycle, but what did it matter? It wasn't as if I had a boyfriend sniffing at my clothes anymore.

It was Sidney Poitier Weekend, and *To Sir, with Love* was playing away on the TV screen with the sound turned off. Sidney Poitier Weekend is always *To Sir, with Love* and nothing else, but I always order a few of his other movies anyway, just to make the whole thing official.

"If it's any consolation, you're much prettier," Derrick said.

"I've seen her, but thanks anyway," I said.

"No, really."

"Derrick, she's an Amazon. She's gorgeous. She's perfect. She's probably exactly what Brian wanted all of those years that he was with me. How shallow of him. How shallow and stupid."

"I think it's more that Anna likes doing outdoorsy stuff. Hiking and climbing, you know? She used to be a guide on Mt. Rainier."

"Oh, God. A happy camper."

"Sorry. God. Here I come over to cheer you up and I'm only making things worse."

"You know what really gets me?"

"What?"

Derrick looked at me. He'd gotten a new haircut since the last time I saw him. It was tightly shorn all over, so that he looked like a bald guy who's recently begun to sprout hair. You could really see every corner of his face this way. And his ears. They were red at the tips, as though he'd just come in from the freezing cold. I had an urge to wrap my palms over those ears, but I didn't want Derrick to think I was making a pass at him. On the TV screen, Sidney Poitier was doing his little frug dance with the luscious Pamela Dare.

"The dog part of it. I mean, a dog! Brian doesn't even like dogs."

"Yeah, I don't know. I don't know about much, really. I've only met her once and she hardly said a word."

"Great. She's quiet, too."

I'd been supplanted by a quiet, mountain-climbing, dog-loving Amazon. Excellent! I couldn't wait to hear what she did for a living.

"She's a vet," Derrick said.

So, fine. So perfect Anna was a vet. Why should that bother me? A woman who is compassionate and dedicated to helping our furry friends in their time of need—how sweet is that?

Okay, it bothered me. A lot. Because it meant that compassionate, dedicated Anna was absolutely everything I wasn't. She probably kept the house clean, too. Couldn't Brian have left me for someone a little less accomplished? A little more confused about her place in the world? It was bad enough that she was beautiful and athletic. Did she have to one-up me in the career department, too? Not that I hadn't made it awfully easy for her to do so.

I wondered if Anna had always wanted to be a veterinarian, if she had dreamed of sewing up dogs and giving vaccines to cats from as far back as she could remember. If she'd practiced on her own little puppy, feeling for lumps in his belly, using her plastic stethoscope to listen for his heartbeat. Or was it an acquired passion? Had she only learned much later in life her affinity for pets or strays—or was it zoo animals she treated? What did they call that kind of vet? A large-animal doctor?

"God, you're a loser," I said to myself.

It was a few weeks after the brunch at my mother's, and I was standing in front of the mirror in my bathroom, watching the way the tears trekked down my cheeks, no instructions necessary. How depressing. Even my tears knew what to do with themselves.

What I needed in that moment was a shove. It didn't even matter in which direction. I couldn't spend the rest of my life standing in front of the bathroom mirror, berating my lack of motivation, while my tears journeyed to the abyss at the base of my chin. Which is one way of explaining how I suddenly found myself deciding to go to synagogue for Yom Kippur, the Day of Atonement. Sin-cleansing day. No eating until sundown. The biggest of all holy days on the Jewish calendar was only two days away—I knew this fact because Alicia, of course, had reminded me, and I, of course, had told her thanks, but no thanks, I don't go to synagogue anymore.

Well, this year, I'd go. It would be a fresh start of sorts. Out with the old, in with the new—that sort of thing. Besides, a little atoning never hurt anybody.

So I called my mother and asked if she had a spare ticket. Since it's the only day all year when nearly all Jews go to services, tickets are required to make sure there are enough seats for the regular dues payers. There's no big Jewish bouncer at the door or anything. But you'd have an awful lot more atoning to do if you showed up and took a seat without a ticket.

"Let me understand this," my mother said to me. "You want to come to services with me?"

"Don't make a big deal out of it. I'm not turning into Alicia or anything."

"Well, thank God for that."

Suffice it to say, my mother wasn't entirely thrilled by Alicia's transformation from pot-smoking carefree youth to wig-adorned hyper-religious matron. Being Jewish was one thing; being religious was something else altogether.

It was a Thursday. Early October. My mother picked me up at my apartment, and when I ran out to the car, I found Ron sitting in the front passenger seat, dressed in a black suit, dark shirt, and tie. He'd slicked back his hair from his forehead. He looked like Johnny Cash with aviator glasses.

"Ronald's coming with us," my mother said with a big smile. God, she was sparkly lately. She had that same shiny orange lipstick on her lips again. She'd gotten herself a new purple trench coat and a pair of sunglasses the size of Utah.

"Oh," I said. "Okay."

I climbed into the backseat, strapped on my seat belt, and looked up at the back of Ron's head. He was wearing a yarmulke, a white one with a circle of navy blue Jewish stars crocheted into the pattern.

"I see you're all ready, Ron," I said to him.

Ron reached up and patted his head. "I'm converting," he said.

"Excuse me?"

"Converting," my mother said. "Ronald's decided to convert."

"You're joking, right?"

My mother shook her head, launching a whorl of citrus-scented perfume through the air and straight up my nose, where it was bound to linger and drive me crazy for the next several hours.

"Not joking, honey. Tell her, Ronald."

Ron shifted his body to take a look at me in the backseat. I hadn't realized before what a large forehead he has. It goes on and on, like a flat desert.

"I have to say, I think this is the right thing for me," Ron said. "Especially if your mother and I decide to, you know, make things legal."

It took me a moment to catch his drift. But then it hit me.

"What?" I said. "You're thinking of getting married?"

My mother peered at me through her rearview mirror.

"We've talked about it," she said.

"You . . . what?" I said. "You've talked about getting married? The two of you? . . . Wow . . . I hardly know what to say. . . . Wow . . . You've been together, what? Three days?"

My mother rolled her eyes. "Six months," she said.

I sat numbly through services, trying to get a grip on this piece of news tossed so breezily in my direction. Impossible!

My mother, marrying again? And more than that, marrying Ron? I stole a quick glance at the two of them sitting next to me—my mother looking ready for a nap, Ron leaning forward eagerly to catch every word from the rabbi's mouth—and suddenly wondered where in the world I'd been the last six months. Because clearly, besides that one Sunday brunch, I'd missed their entire romance. Had they really been together for half a year? I guess I'd been so wrapped up in the end of my own relationship that I hadn't noticed the beginning of my mother's. I felt kind of bad about that.

I edged over so that I could whisper into my mother's ear.

"Does Dad know?"

"Know what?"

"You know. About you and Ron. Getting married."

"Don't get worked up. We're just talking."

I didn't hear a thing the rabbi said. I sat in the wooden pew, wondering if there were any chance in hell I'd be written into the Book of Life for the following year. That's the deal on Yom Kippur: You either get written into the Book of Life for the next twelve months or you don't. Atoning gives you better odds.

*Okay,* the voice in my head said, even though I had my doubts that anybody was listening. *Okay, I'm sorry I didn't notice that my mother was*—I could barely summon the words—*falling in love. With Ron, of all people.*

I hoped that was good enough. Because the second I got home from services, I made myself a big tuna sandwich, and even though it wouldn't be dark for hours and hours, I sat on the sofa and ate the whole thing.

I told myself that I wouldn't drive past Brian's house anymore. It was ridiculous. What could possibly come of it? It was only a form of self-torture, good for nothing but lowering my self-esteem to new personal record levels. Still, I couldn't give it up. I told myself that at least I wasn't calling him, or writing him incessant e-mails, or mailing him Barbie and Ken dolls with tiny arrows through the head, or kidnapping him and keeping him locked up in a basement somewhere. I was only driving past his house, out of curiosity's sake. Not completely sane, but not completely crazy, either.

Until it did get crazy. Because later that same afternoon—after my mother's news and the tuna sandwich—I found myself stopping in front of his house. Without consciously deciding to do it, I put the car into park, set the brake, rolled down the window, and turned off the engine. I don't know what got into me, exactly. I think my mother and Ron's almost-engagement had finally put me over the edge. I sat in front of Brian's house hoping that somehow Brian would telepathically get the message that I was just outside, thinking bad thoughts about him. And then he'd come out and climb into my car and we'd drive away, leaving Anna the veterinarian to her dog.

But he didn't come out of the house. No one came out of the house. Nothing happened at all. This total lack of movement didn't sit well with me. Where was everybody? And why was it that they were all out—most likely having a goddamned good time—while I was miserable? There was something terribly wrong with the entire equation.

On the front lawn, a couple of white-water kayaks lay upside down. Brian had spent a whole summer a few years back trying to teach me how to white-water kayak. He'd been very patient, actually, flipping my kayak over in Lake Washington as practice for a river and telling me I had to count to five while holding my breath underwater before I could rip off the rubber protective skirt and climb out of the boat. I never made it past two. I'm not a big fan of death by drowning.

Maybe Brian and I hadn't really belonged together. Yes, I was permanently—probably stupidly—in love with the guy, but when you got right down to it, we'd had almost nothing in common. Not our religions, not our temperaments, not the things we liked to do. I used to like to think our differences made us one of those interesting, opposites-attract kind of couples, but as it turned out, maybe we really weren't all that interesting. We were only different. Two very different people who in truth probably fought a bit too much in between sleeping together.

And now Brian was sleeping with somebody else. Well, something needed to be done.

I got out of the car. I walked to the side of the house where the dog was kept in his outdoor kennel. I saw the dog lying inside his doghouse, asleep.

"Hey, dog," I said.

He opened his eyes and looked at me. I unlatched the gate to his enclosure.

"Here, boy."

The dog lifted himself up. He was a big dog. And awfully hairy. He sauntered over to where I stood and sniffed at my leg.

"Hey, big guy," I said again. I had no idea how a person talked to a dog. "How are you doing?"

The dog pushed past me. He didn't seem too overwhelmed by his sudden taste of freedom. He seemed more bored than anything. This dog needed a little excitement in his life.

I walked to my car and opened the front passenger seat. The dog leapt in. He sat on the seat like he'd been riding in my car for years. He looked at me. I figured I had about eight more hours to atone for what I was about to do before the gates slammed closed on Yom Kippur. I shut the door.

"Good boy," I said.

Sick as this may sound, I couldn't help but take pride in my doggy-kidnapping escapade. Finally, I'd done something a person could write home about, if writing home about stealing a dog from an old boyfriend's new girlfriend was something a person felt like writing home about. Up until I swiped the Big Guy, the most outlandish thing I'd ever done was dancing on top of a piano in a bar in Portland, an event I don't even have the embarrassing pleasure of remembering but which I've been assured was quite elaborate and extended.

Oh, and I used to shoplift now and again. And of course, the drugs. But overall, I've led a pretty clean and calm life. So I told myself that a nice pat on the back at my newfound bandit status was well deserved. No need to feel like slitting my wrists at my own stupidity.

In fact, that night I let the Big Guy sleep with me. Actually, I had no choice in the matter. He showed not a whit of interest in the fluffy orange beach towel I'd laid out for him on the floor by the radiator. And every time I kicked him off my bed, he only leapt back up again. Finally I gave up. As it turned out, the Big Guy was a lot more polite than some guys I could speak of. He didn't hog the entire bed by sleeping at an angle, relegating me to a miniature triangle of mattress for the night, for instance. He didn't turn over in his sleep and take all of the covers with him. He didn't ask if maybe I'd neglected to brush my teeth. No, compared with some people who shall remain nameless, he was quite the gentleman.

# 4

Despite his lack of knowledge in certain areas—the proper way to break up with one's fiancée, for example—Brian had always known one thing for certain: No matter what he ended up doing to support himself, it would inevitably have some kind of connection to the great outdoors. To that end, he studied forestry in college, spent summers hauling non-climbers up Mt. Rainier and nonrafters down rivers in Idaho, and eventually found himself employed at an outdoor-clothing company in Seattle, helping to design and market the company's wares.

Meanwhile, I was waiting tables.

Of course, I didn't grow up planning to be a waitress. I'd planned on being a movie star, with my face plastered all over billboards and my name in magazines and a couple of Oscars sitting on the mantelpiece of the mansion I'd own in Hollywood, complete with swimming pool, lounge chairs, and a host of maids in little white aprons serving iced drinks on silver trays. In anticipation of my stardom, I worked diligently throughout my childhood on my Oscar-winning speech, a speech whose content changed nightly depending on the state of my current friendships, or whether I was mad at my mom, dad, or Alicia, or whether I felt the need to make some type of political pitch, like when Sacheen Littlefeather showed up instead of Marlon Brando to say he was refusing the award because of the way Hollywood treated Indians. Of course, number one on my list of internationally heard and coveted thank-yous would be the talent scout who would walk into my classroom at Dwight Allen Elementary School and immediately recognize my charm, grace, and untapped talent and sign me right up. By that afternoon, I'd be a star and have to make Oscar acceptance speeches while wearing a fabulous gown. And I'd have a fabulous and handsome hairdresser on Oscar night, too, one who would know the trick for magically sweeping my unruly hair into a neat, smooth bun. I had it all down perfectly. The award, the gown, the speech. Now all I needed was some actual acting.

"Honey," my mother said to me, "it's wonderful that you want to be a movie star. But I have to tell you. You're not all that comfortable onstage."

Not all that comfortable onstage? What did that have to do with it? My troubling tendency to pee my pants before public presentations of any sort had *nothing* to do with the movies. Movies had *cuts*. Movies had *editors*. Movies were shot without audiences of parents watching your every move, making you so nervous that you felt you might pee in your pants. Movies were *movies.*

"Okay, you'll be a movie star," my mother said. "Remember to thank your mother in your Oscar speech."

What did she think I'd been doing, night after night after night? Of course I'd thank my mother. All the movie stars thanked their mothers. In fact, the whole reason I even wanted to be a movie star was so that I could win an Oscar and give my Oscar speech and thank my mother and everybody else. The acting part of it was only one trivial detail in the entire plan.

"I'll consider it," I told her.

And I would have, too, except for the fact that the talent scout never showed.

My early dream of stardom dashed, I waited for a new dream to appear. Elementary school came and went, middle and high schools. No dream. College arrived, and still nothing had come to me. I took course after course, hoping some subject flying around in the universe would dive-bomb into my life and reveal my true calling. But after four years, not the slightest blip had registered on my radar screen. I was a person without a passion, doomed to spend my years in unsatisfying jobs while everyone around me followed their bliss.

When finally I made up my mind to become a speech therapist in an elementary school, I was seriously relieved. It seemed like such a good, practical plan at the time. Summers off, same Thanksgiving and Christmas vacations as the ones

I'd had my entire life, a regular paycheck. Besides, what else was I going to do with the English degree I'd managed to eke out? I congratulated myself on such forward thinking, applied to graduate school around the same time I met Brian, and then dug right in, determined to devote myself to a career I cared nothing about.

As part of my training, I did a half-semester stint at an elementary school in north Seattle. One day, my supervisor at the school took me aside. She was a nice old lady—Mrs. Gernel—very organized, always bustling about with a pencil tucked behind an ear. A wearer of sensible shoes and buttoned-up cardigans. She was the type who always had a good piece of advice for you, whether you asked for it or not.

"Rena," she said, "do you mind if I ask you a question?"

"Sure," I said. "What is it?"

"Well, I've been wondering. This may sound kind of strange, but . . . well . . . do you like kids?"

Did I like kids? Wasn't I devoting my adult life to helping children?

"I like kids," I said. "Of course I like kids."

But right then, as I spoke the words, I knew it wasn't true. I didn't particularly like kids.

"Oh, all right, then," Mrs. Gernel said. "That's wonderful."

I finished out the half semester, wondering what in God's name I'd gotten myself into. And then I had a flash of brilliance. I'd work with adults. Adults needed speech therapists, didn't they? Adults who'd suffered strokes or brain trauma?

Adults who were developmentally disabled? Adults who still lisped into their thirties? Surely I'd enjoy working with grown-ups.

I did my next half semester at a downtown hospital. Needless to say, working with adults suffering from strokes or brain trauma is a fast trip down misery lane. I could barely summon the inner strength to face my clients, sad day after sad day. These humans, who only weeks before had led vital and energetic lives, now were destined to live out their days in various modes of disability. It was heartbreaking.

I quit graduate school, rambled through a series of menial jobs that made me almost wish I hadn't nixed the speech therapy career, and finally, a few years ago, ended up waiting tables at Sammy's Place, a steak joint in downtown Seattle. Turned out carrying five platters on one arm, remembering a table full of complicated dinner orders, and dealing with the multitudes of ill-mannered diners among us came naturally to me. And that's it. I'd been there ever since.

When I woke up Friday morning, I had one glorious moment when I thought the whole doggy-snatching thing was a dream. A very funny dream, because as if I would be so stupid as to steal my old boyfriend's new girlfriend's dog! Ridiculous! Only a complete idiot would do such a terrible thing and think she could get away with it!

Then the Big Guy shoved his big face into my sleepy one and licked me straight across the mouth. I pushed the dog away and checked the clock. Only ten A.M. Ever since Brian had vanished, I'd found that the longer I slept, the less time there was left over to face the day. It was quite brilliant, really. A couple of times, early on, I'd shown such dedication to the plan that I didn't get out of bed at all. If only I could apply myself with such enthusiasm to just about anything else—preferably something that paid big bucks—I'd be on to something.

The Big Guy was very patient. He sat next to me on the bed, panting and staring me in the eye. Really staring. Kind of freak-me-out sort of staring. Each time I looked at him, he was looking right back at me. I closed my eyes and counted to ten, opened them, and sure enough, his big eyes still gazed into mine. I laughed crazily. He stared. I stuck out my tongue. He stared. I turned my head in the other direction and then turned it back toward him—quick!—and still he stared. The dog was a staring machine.

"You looking at me?" I asked him. I do a terrible De Niro. "You looking at me?"

The Big Guy was silent as the Buddha and just as nonjudgmental, a quality I looked for in my own heart without success when I realized he'd taken a dump in the middle of the room.

Obviously, the dog was going to have to go immediately back to its rightful owner. That was a given. This little shenanigan had been tons of fun—for me, anyway—but all fun and games must eventually come to an end. Of course, when I made off with the dog I hadn't given a moment's thought as to how I would put him back again. It occurred to me then that returning the dog was probably going to be way more difficult than stealing him had been in the first place. Returning the dog ran the risk of being caught and then having to somehow explain why I'd ever thought to do such a stupid thing. I'd rather be pinned by a boulder and have to cut off my own arm to escape than explain why in the world I was shooing the Big Guy back into his little pen at three in the morning.

And yet something was going to have to be done. My apartment smelled exactly like dog shit, and with very good reason. More than that, the Big Guy had already chewed up one of my favorite slippers and was halfway through chewing up its mate. I was more amazed than ever that people call dogs "man's best friend." Do best friends destroy your things? Perhaps "man's best friend" is meant to be ironic. Perhaps it's a message that sometimes your best friend can turn out to do bad things, like reach into your chest and rip out your still beating heart and then drop it on the floor and do a little dance on top of it. Things like that.

And then there was that other niggling detail I'd been trying my best to overlook: the illegal angle of my escapade. Look, I may not be the most knowledgeable Jew in the world, but it didn't take a bacon-shunning Hasid to know "Thou shalt not steal" is right up there in the top ten list of commandments. My conscience was having a heart attack.

I scrounged around in my refrigerator, looking for something a dog might consider food. Probably not a near empty jar of mayo, a foil-wrapped former half burrito purchased at some point in the distant past, two dried-up apples, or a liter of flat Diet Coke. No, my refrigerator held nothing a dog could, say, eat, much less a person. And I was all out of tuna fish—the dog had downed my last can the night before. Finally, I found a box of Wheat Thins in the cupboard and split them with the Big Guy. Then I cracked open the liter of flat Diet Coke and called Lisa.

"Guess what?" I said.

"Hold on."

Lisa is a dying breed in that she still smokes. No one's supposed to know. She's been trying to quit for about fifteen years. At Sammy's Place, she smokes in the dark and always smelly kitchen bathroom, leaving her still lit butts in an ashtray on the sink between serving customers. If smoking in the most disgusting bathroom in Seattle can't get her to quit, I doubt anything will. I could hear her lighting a match through the phone receiver.

If only I were a smoker, too. All of that black tar and nicotine burning through my lungs, cutting short my meaningless existence. Of course, with my luck, I'd probably get cancer of the jaw and have to walk around for a couple of years with half my face missing before taking my final breath. And what if those two years were the same two years when I finally discovered my personal meaning in life and that personal meaning turned out to entail public speaking? Better to not smoke cigarettes and stick to other, similarly pleasing yet less life-threatening vices. Of which there are none.

"Okay, shoot," she said.

"I got a dog."

"You got a dog."

"I got a dog."

"You don't like animals."

"That's the old me. The new me loves dogs."

"Since when?"

"Since I got him."

"And what brought this on?"

"God, can't a person get a dog without the big interrogation over it?"

The Big Guy seemed awfully interested in my Diet Coke. I poked through my sink of dirty dishes until a bowl materialized, filled the bowl with water, and put it on the floor. The Big Guy lapped up the whole bowlful in five seconds flat, leaving a smattering of water droplets on the floor. I filled the bowl with Diet Coke.

"What kind is he?"

"I don't know."

"How can you not know?"

"Our love isn't dependent on breed. It's more pure than that."

"What's his name?"

"Big Guy."

"That's not a name."

"You are exhausting me."

"I'll be right over."

# 5

Among the zillions of things I didn't take into account when I made off with the dog was the fact that dogs are not allowed in my apartment building. I hadn't noticed the sign before on the front door: NO DOGS ALLOWED. You'd think I would have seen it, seeing as how I'd lived in the building for nine long years and gone in and out of the front door of the building probably five times a day over those nine years, and if you were the type to add up whatever that adds up to, you'd come up with a very large number. But, no, I never saw it. When you don't have a dog that you wish to be allowed into the building, you don't notice the NO DOGS ALLOWED sign. But now, pseudo dog owner that I was, I suddenly noticed it.

This was a big problem. It was bad enough to worry about Derrick catching me red-handed—a distinct possibility, especially with his tendency to drop by at odd hours, hoping for that sexual favor that was never going to come his way.

But even if I somehow managed to slip past Derrick, it was only a matter of time before Carl, the super of the building, nabbed me. All of which accounted for the secret spy action I had to take every time the Big Guy needed to go out. Let me tell you in case you've never tried it yourself: It's awfully difficult to covertly make it down three flights of stairs and then back up again with a dog the size of a Volkswagen.

The thing was, Carl wasn't your typical vanishing act of a super, the kind who's never available when the hot water mysteriously disappears or the washing machine suddenly decides to flood. No, Carl was ever-present and all-knowing. Not only was Carl's apartment situated on the first floor right between the front door and the alcove at the bottom of the stairs, but Carl himself was often—seemingly always—situated between the front door and the little alcove at the bottom of the stairs. It was nearly impossible to make it in or out of the building without literally running into the hovering, ancient, and endlessly talking Carl, with his endless supply of long, tangent-filled tutorials on one topic or another. You'd have thought that, at eighty-eight, he might need a moment to rest his tired legs or, at the very least, his ragged vocal cords. But Carl had a purpose in life: to keep his one-man constant vigil in the foyer going for as long as humanly possible. The guy should have gotten a medal for such intense dedication. Instead, he got a steady stream of residents racing by or cutting him off midsentence with some flimsy excuse for running out the door. The beauty of Carl was that he never seemed to mind, or even to notice. What he did mind, however, was anyone purposely disobeying building rules, and in particular the rule about dogs, a rule he'd taken the time and effort to post on the front door in plain sight.

"Whose dog is that?" he barked at me.

He gave me his patented wild and shocked look, as though I had mistakenly appeared in the foyer without any clothes on. As always, his white hair stood at attention at the top of his head. A former military man, Carl had never turned his back on the crew cut of his youth, nor did he see any reason to vary from his daily uniform of green pants and stained white shirts, cinched in the middle by a black leather belt. He looked exactly like a skeleton with clothes.

"What, this dog?" I said.

Carl pointed a long, bent finger, so that the tip aimed straight for the dog. The rest of his finger formed a neat arch, like a rainbow.

"Yes, this dog," he said.

"He's not mine."

"Don't matter whose he is or isn't. You see that sign there?"

Carl shifted his stance so that his bent finger no longer pointed at the dog, but instead pointed in the general direction of the front door.

"Yes."

"What's it say?"

"No dogs allowed."

Carl folded his arms across his skinny, caved-in chest, victorious.

"That's right," he said. "No. Dogs. Allowed."

"I'm actually taking him out of here right now. We're on our way out. See? Here we go. Out the door." I scooted past Carl toward the front door of the building. "Okay, we're out of here!"

"No dogs!" Carl yelled after me.

Time for Plan B, I told myself. Unfortunately, there was no Plan B. Fortunately, I knew better than to believe there were any true consequences to my blatant rule breaking. Carl was a pushover. Besides, over the years we'd established a little routine: I'd run out and retrieve burgers and fries from his favorite takeout spot a couple of times a month, and in return, well, there really wasn't much I got in return except the mitzvah points. The thing is, when you're not big in the volunteer department—no banging nails for Habitat for Humanity, for example; no writing letters for Amnesty International—you've got to grab your good deeds where you can find them. Carl would nab the bag and his change from my hand, always acting as though I hadn't done him any big favors. But in truth, I knew he appreciated it. In other words, Carl liked me.

"It's my sister's. She needed someone to watch him. She's . . . sick! He'll be gone in a few days. I think," I said.

I really had no idea.

"No matter. No dogs!"

"Bring you back a Dick's Special and a chocolate milkshake? My treat?"

Carl scratched at his bony head with his long fingers.

"Large fries?" I asked. "Extra order of special sauce?"

"You've got one week, tops," he said.

And that seemed to settle things for everybody.

When Lisa says she'll be right over, nine times out of ten she's never going to show. But this time she really did head right over. Not expecting her, I was outside, walking the dog and hoping he'd take a shit before my toes froze off. I'd put the ugly purple collar back on him, and to that I'd tied the belt from my blue terry-cloth robe for a leash.

"Let's go, Big Guy," I told him. "Let's go, let's go, let's go, let's go, let's go, let's go, let's go, let's go, let's go, let's go, let's go, let's go, let's go, let's go, let's go."

Lisa pulled up in her boyfriend's station wagon. She rolled down the window.

"It's a yellow lab," she said.

"Mystery solved!"

"Nice leash, Martha Stewart. So, who'd you steal him from?"

"Brian."

Lisa stared at me. "No," she said.

"Just kidding."

"You're not."

"I'm not."

"You stole Brian's dog?"

"Actually I'm pretty sure it must be Brian's new girlfriend's dog. Brian doesn't really like animals."

"Brian's girlfriend?"

"Yeah."

"You stole her dog?"

"Yeah."

"Oh, man. Are you in trouble."

The Big Guy did his business, and Lisa watched while I thrust my hand inside a plastic bag and surgically plucked his excrement from the grass. I flipped the bag around, made a neat little package of the plastic bag, and held it at arm's length like a flag of surrender. Then I walked it the few yards to the garbage bin on the street corner and tossed it in.

"I can't believe I just saw you do that," Lisa said.

"Help me take him back?"

Lisa sighed. Then she smiled at me, a smile that's all pink gums with a row of lovely white teeth thrown in seemingly as an afterthought. It's a killer smile. Lisa's one of those beautiful types whose beauty goes completely unnoticed until one day when you finally take a really good look behind the black glasses and the bird's-nest hairdo to find she has perfect skin and tiny, angelic features.

"You are *so* fucked up," she said.

I put the dog in the backseat of the station wagon, shoved in next to him, and we all headed toward Brian's, me convinced for one wild instant that I could sneak the Big Guy back into his pen before anyone noticed he was missing and Lisa telling me how stupid I was to think such a thing was possible.

"Maybe they haven't checked on him yet," I said.

Lisa shook her head. "You're confusing Brian's new girlfriend with yourself."

She was right, of course. Only someone as irresponsible as yours truly would have neglected to check on her own dog for twenty-four hours. I looked at the dog.

"They've checked on you, baby. I know they have."

"You're calling him 'baby' now?"

"Don't make fun of me."

"Oh, right. Don't make fun of you. Sure. That dog better not pee on the seat."

A couple of blocks later, she slammed on the brakes.

"Look," she said. She pointed to a sign printed on purple paper with black lettering and stapled to a telephone pole. They knew he was gone all right.

**WHERE'S TILLY?**

Yellow labrador.

Four years old.

Last seen wearing purple collar.

Reward for return!

No questions asked!

They must have been up all night, Brian and Anna, stapling signs to telephone poles, taping them to newspaper boxes and storefronts, slipping flyers under windshield wipers of parked cars for blocks on end. What mutual purpose I'd provided that whacky pair of young lovers! And yet, something told me that if I were to openly return the former Tilly at that moment, not only would there be no reward awaiting me, but the promise of no questions would be flushed right down the toilet along with my head.

Fortunately, Brian's new neighborhood and my neighborhood were separated by at least a couple of other neighborhoods, making the chances of someone seeing the signs, seeing me with the Big Guy, and then putting two and two together pretty close to nil. Still, I've never been the type to let good odds interfere with my tendency toward paranoia. Worst-case scenarios had already played out in my brain, complete with flashing police lights, dimly lit jail cells, and unsentimental judges. I'd told myself that women's prisons weren't nearly as bad as men's, that maybe as an inmate I might finally do something with myself—teach other inmates to read, for instance. Get a law degree behind bars. Why, getting thrown in the slammer may turn out to be the very thing an unmotivated gal like me needed, if only I didn't lack the motivation to test the theory.

"You ready?" Lisa said.

She took the turn onto Cascade Boulevard and slowly made her way up the street toward Brian's house, while I sank down low in the backseat with the dog.

"Do you see anything?" I asked.

"No."

"How about now? Do you see anything now?"

"No. Shut up. I'm looking."

"You're driving too slow. It looks suspicious to go so slow."

"Shut. Up."

"What do you see?"

"Shhhh. I see something."

"What? What is it?"

Lisa pressed on the gas. "The happy couple. On the front porch."

"Oh, shit."

"I'm going to the end of the block and turning around. You stay down."

"Why are you turning around? Don't turn around! Why are you turning around?"

"Do you want to get rid of the dog or not?"

"Yes! But not when they're on the front porch!"

"Open the door and let him out. They'll find him."

"I'm not going to just let him out. What if he runs away?"

"What do you care? God, you're driving me crazy. Open the door."

"Drive by again."

Lisa took a deep breath and blew it out. Then she pulled into a driveway, turned the car around, and headed back down Cascade.

"Oh, God. Get a load of this," she said a moment later.

"What?"

"Just peek. They won't see you."

"Are you positive?"

"Hurry up."

I lifted my head just far enough to get a peek at my old boyfriend pressing his body against the body of his new girlfriend, which was itself pressed up against the front door of the house. I couldn't be certain, but it seemed possible the Amazon was wearing a pair of shorts she'd purchased in the preteen department at Macy's. Size negative four or something.

"Are they making out?" I said.

"I'd say they are."

"In public?"

"It's their front porch."

They were really going at it, one long, intense kiss for all the world to see. If only I'd had a rifle on me, I could have taken them both down with a single shot through their doubled-up midsections.

"Oh, for fuck's sake," I said.

Just then, Brian's hands dropped from Anna's neck to her waist. As I watched in escalating horror, he made a little dipping action in the knees, lifted her into the air as though she were a ballerina, and then let her fold her long legs around his waist, pretzel-like. Now that was going too far! He used to lift *me* that way! Okay, so my much shorter legs didn't execute quite such a perfect pretzel around Brian's perfect middle. Still! I was the goddamn ballerina!

"Oh, God. I'm going to puke," I said.

"No puking in Peter's car."

"Let's get out of here."

"What about the dog?"

"Well, I can't exactly return him right now."

"Two minutes and they'll be inside doing the nasty on the living room rug."

"That's very comforting," I said.

Lisa drove to the end of the block and pulled over.

"What do you want to do?" she asked.

I didn't really have to think about it.

"I'm keeping the dog," I said.

# 6

Brian wasn't always an asshole. In fact, he could often be very sweet, especially when I got bad haircuts and he'd tell me they weren't so bad, or the times when I had the flu or a bad cold and he'd make me chicken soup (from a can, but still) and bring me pillows and blankets and magazines. Or when he used to let me place my ice-cube feet between his thighs to warm them at night, even though there are few things worse than another person's freezing cold feet against your warm thighs in the middle of the night. Or when he'd go out and get us both lattes on Sunday mornings while I slept and bring mine back to me in bed.

Other things, too. He insisted I looked good in the lingerie that he used to buy me (online) for Valentine's Day and insisted I looked even better with the lingerie removed. He was always smiling at me from across the room at parties and telling me later that I was the prettiest girl in the room. He laughed at my jokes, and not to be nice, but because he really thought I was funny. Sometimes he'd stare at me when he thought I wasn't looking.

Once when he went out of town on a climbing trip, I came home to find, under the covers of my bed, several pieces of old cardboard ripped up and taped back together to more or less resemble a life-size body, the words *I love you* written next to the mouth.

Like my personal Mr. Rogers, he used to tell me he loved me exactly the way I was. And I think he tried really hard to mean it, too. But when you got right down to it, exactly the way I was left a lot to be desired. For Brian, anyway.

By Friday afternoon—after buying some really bad-smelling dog food and a cheap leash and taking the Big Guy outside twenty times so that he could torment me by not peeing or pooping on the little patch of grass outside my building because he preferred to pee or poop in the privacy of my apartment instead—stealing the dog was once again beginning to seem like one of the stupider things I'd ever done. And I've done a lot of stupid things. And yet, I couldn't decide: Sneak the dog back to his pen? Keep him? Take him to the pound? Tell Brian the whole thing and hope he'd see the humor in all of it? If only I were the type of person who could actually make decisions, everything would be perfect—I'd decide what to do with the dog and then do it. Unfortunately, I spend a great deal of my life avoiding making decisions. Besides, before any further doggy decisions could be conceived of—

much less acted upon—I had to make it through Friday night dinner at Alicia and Aryeh's, with my mother and Ron.

Under most circumstances, eating food that I don't have to prepare on dishes that are not my responsibility to wash afterward would throw me into fits of joy. But going to Friday night dinner at Alicia's is not "most circumstances." Going to Friday night dinner at Alicia's is a small form of torture, as it means doing the entire Jewish Sabbath rigmarole and all the while doing my best to pretend I'm enjoying such an opportunity. Not that I ever fool my sister.

It's difficult to imagine now, but before Alicia became Aviva, married Aryeh, plunked a wig over her own lovely head of pitch-black curls, and started full-time baby production, she was a very dedicated pot smoker. In fact, she pretty well paid her way through her Oregon college by dealing Baggies of weed, first from her freshman dorm room and later from the house she shared with her circle of stoner friends. Whether Aryeh knows anything about his wife's prior lucrative career in the herb business, I don't know. But then, Aryeh wasn't always Aryeh, either. Perhaps he was a drug dealer in an earlier life, too.

How my sister became religious is something I don't entirely understand. All I know is that midway through the year she was taking off before starting grad school (hard to believe now, but she'd majored in women's studies), she suddenly caught a flight home, walked into her old bedroom, dropped her things, and went to bed. Apparently, she'd suffered a traumatic breakup with an Oregon boyfriend none of us had been aware of, triggering a supersize bout of depression. Or maybe it was something else that brought her down—she never talks about the specifics. All I know is that nothing could rouse my sister from her stupor. My parents tried everything, everything being food, offers of therapy, and mostly lots of head shaking at the situation. Finally, they put her on a plane headed for Israel. A few months in a kibbutz—that was all Alicia needed to recover from whatever it was she needed recovering from. Of course, they hoped she'd come home less interested in weed and more interested in finding herself a Jewish boyfriend. Not in a million years did they think she'd find religion, even in the Holy Land. To everyone's shock (and horror), she returned from her trip as Aviva, headed directly for the little Orthodox shul near my parents' house, was quickly fixed up by the happy congregation with the eligible and newly Orthodox Aryeh, and the rest is history. I hear this type of thing happens all the time—religious conversions of such a total nature. I just never would have believed it would happen to Alicia.

I gave the Big Guy a little lecture before I left.

"Do not chew on anything but this!" I said, handing him a rawhide bone. "Do not pee in a corner of my closet. Do not bark uncontrollably at birds flying past the window. Do not scratch like a maniac on the door to be let out."

I couldn't think of anything else, so I gave him a few pats on the back and then kissed the top of his head.

"Good *Shabbos*!" I said.

---

I walked into Alicia's house without knocking, slipped off my shoes, and hung my jacket on a hook by the door. Someone had already taped the light switch in the foyer to the "on" position. Among a few thousand other rules, you're not allowed to flick light switches on the Sabbath if you're Orthodox, so Alicia tapes the ones she wants to stay on. Those Orthodox think of everything.

Ron was in the living room, wearing a new yarmulke. A green one this time, with white Hebrew lettering stitched into the rim. He pulled it off to show me.

"It says 'Ro-nee,'" he said, pointing at the Hebrew letters as though maybe I'd learned something in Hebrew school—Hebrew, for instance—and could read the letters on his little green skullcap. "My Hebrew name."

"Nice," I said.

"Your mother made it for me."

This was another new one. My mother making crafts. Never in my life had I seen my mother involved in anything *close* to crafty. Sewing machine? No such thing in the house. Knitting needles? Just buy a sweater! She'd never so much as threaded a simple needle to hem a pair of pants. That's why there was a Naomi at that little tailor shop on 75th Street. So that you could take your pants to her to be hemmed. This sudden immersion in the world of crochet was going to take some readjustment of neural pathways through the mother corner of my brain. The mother I'd grown up with had no domestic skills to speak of. On the other hand, she'd always been an expert on vaginas, birth control methods, STDs, Pap smears, breast exams, abortion services, masturbation, yeast infections, and just about anything else imaginable in the between-the-legs category. Unlike the other mothers, all of whom seemed to be busying themselves throughout my childhood volunteering to chaperone field trips, or baking treats for post–soccer game festivities, or having normal avoidance-filled conversations about sexuality with their children instead of delivering dissertations on the subject, my mother was all tied up dispensing therapy at the local Planned Parenthood. By the time I turned twelve and developed the breast buds I'd heard so much about, having a mother with such a vast pool of sexual knowledge no longer seemed normal. It was more like suddenly noticing your mother doesn't have a nose. Frightening. Not to mention embarrassing.

Now, my mother stood next to Ron, smiling with pride. She'd gotten a new haircut, one that left her with a hank of bangs that fell in a straight line over her eyes. The short navy skirt had made a return engagement, but fortunately, she'd killed the boots, replacing them this time with a pair of sensible black shoes. I have to admit, she actually looked pretty good.

"Since when do you know how to crochet?" I asked her.

"Ronald taught me," she said.

"I could teach *you,* if you'd like," Ron said to me. "You could make someone a yarmulke."

I looked at my mother, who had tilted her face earthward to peer up at me with raised eyebrows, which was her way of telling me to be nice.

"Sure," I said to Ron. "That would be great!"

Ron set the yarmulke back on top of his head, and my mother reached up and clipped it into place with a little silver hair clip.

"There!" she said. "Doesn't that look sharp!"

"Next thing you know, you'll be keeping kosher," I said.

My mother pointed a finger at me. It's amazing just how much mileage my mother can squeeze out of a single pointed finger, even when she's not using her middle one.

Just at that moment, a slew of small children dashed through the living room, made a couple of leaping, twisting circles on and about the furniture, and then dashed back out again, all the while screaming some crazy Hebrew song at the top of their lungs. Alicia's children have exactly two modes: movement and sleep. When sleep isn't in the offing, they go into full movement mode, running and jumping and most of all screaming from all corners of the house. Somehow, Alicia and Aryeh don't notice. They never do. Either it's cultural or the Orthodox simply don't have a chapter in the Torah on parenting skills. If I ever bothered to read the Good Book, I suppose I'd know for sure.

Oh, the superiority of the childless. Nothing makes us happier about our own carefree childless existence than noisy, raving, dancing, spitting children. I'm quite certain that when and if the day comes that a baby magically falls—without pain—from between my legs, I will be the first to pronounce noisy children God's gift to the world, and my own offspring, in particular, God's very favorite noisy gift. But no such thing has happened yet, and so, as I stood there in Alicia's living room, I wanted nothing more than for someone to yell out for the kids to sit down and shut up.

In an event that can only mean there really is a God and He'd chosen this moment to prove to me His existence, my father, king of the tell-kids-what-to-do kingdom, suddenly appeared.

"Dad!" I said. "I didn't know you were coming!"

"Hello, sweetie," he said.

"Hello, Al," my mother said.

"Hello, Helen. Hello, Ron."

"Hello, Al," Ron said.

The kids raced through again, this time grabbing on to the legs of the adults and laughing.

"Now, now," my mother said.

"Inside voices," Ron said.

"Hands off the merchandise," I said in as nice a tone as I could muster.

*"Everybody slow down!"* my father hollered, at which point the children fell on the floor in hysterics.

My father's sole parenting skills, carried down from his father before him and honed ever more precisely on his two daughters during their formative years, consists of three distinct techniques. The first, and most often employed, involves hollering at whoever happens to be in the vicinity to either "slow down," "relax," "calm down," or "be quiet." Activity level of the recipient of such instruction has no bearing. You can be peacefully watching television, say, or reading a book, or doing absolutely nothing discernible at all. You can be locked in deep meditation, your body still as stone. Somewhere deep inside, so deep inside that you aren't even aware of it yet, my father knows you are considering making motion. Better to nip it in the bud with a quick holler of, "Calm down!" before things get out of hand. "Be quiet" is perhaps the most widely used of his instructions, although he doesn't use those particular words, preferring instead the single-syllable, earsplitting blast of *"Shah!!!"* which, as children, we soon learned meant the same thing.

Second in my father's repertoire is the stare-down. Chin low, eyes like laser beams, his mouth a straight, hard line, my father holds the Guinness world record for length of time employed while holding the stare. Pity the poor imp with the nerve to say something off-color, or to come home with a bad report card, or to refuse to eat their peas. My father's stark, intensive stare could have blown the mustache off of Hitler himself. Small children don't stand a chance.

And then there is the coup de grâce. The stomp. Only the most egregious behavior merits use of the stomp. One foot and then the other, over and over, crashing down on the kitchen floor, out one door, down the hallway, and back into the kitchen through the other door, circle after circle, all the while accompanied by a howl, and then a moan, and then a howl again, as though whatever you've done has somehow taken hold of his internal organs and wrenched them irretrievably out of place. The stomp, the howl, the look of intense pain: My father has locked up the corner on nonviolent discipline. Not a hand raised. Not a moment's threat of physical contact. And yet the stomp says it all: You have done a terrible thing from which you may never recover.

Of course, by the time Alicia and I had passed from childhood to adolescence, the holler, the stare, and even the stomp had passed their glory days and moved inexorably toward teasing imitation. My father was left no choice but to change tactics in order to keep his daughters in line. Unfortunately, he had no new tactics to employ, and his parenting skills took a precipitous dive off the cliff of effectiveness. It wasn't until years later that he revealed one final trick up his sleeve, a psychological trick he'd been saving—without his conscious knowledge—until absolutely necessary. My breakup with Brian finally provided him with just such an opportunity.

"I don't understand it," he said to me after I broke the news. "I sent you to college so that you could get a job, so you could buy some nice clothes, so you could go to nice places, so you could meet a nice boy and marry him. What happened?"

I didn't know where to begin with such a question. Even my mother—who was supposed to be more progressive about such things—wished nothing more for me than a husband with a decent job and a high sperm count. No wonder I'd never known what to do with my life. I'd been raised with a singular mandate to provide grandchildren to my parents.

"Dad," I said. "Please."

"Look, is it so wrong that I want you to be happy?"

I looked at my dad. What could I say? Of course he wanted me to be happy.

"I just think there are other routes to happiness besides meeting a guy," I said to him. But even as I said it, deep down I doubted it was true—at least for me. My happiness depended on loving someone and being loved back. God, my parents' juju had done its trick, a thought nearly as depressing as my newly established single state. Still, wanting to love someone and being loved in return—it's not as though that's a terrible thing to wish on someone.

"Name one," he said.

If only I could come up with an answer, perhaps I could convince us both.

"What about a person's job?" I said. "Can't a person's job bring them happiness?"

Al shrugged. "A job you love is a kind of happiness," he said.

We were both silent for a moment. I was pretty certain we were both thinking the same thing. I was a waitress. It wasn't bringing me a whole lot of happiness. My dad put a hand on my shoulder and smiled at me.

"Come work with me," he said. "Really. Give it a try. If you don't like it, no problem. There's always another restaurant job out there."

I'd heard this same pitch from my dad a few thousand times before. He'd given up on Alicia ever joining the family business the day she put on the wig and became Aviva, but he still had a few slivers of hope that daughter number two would find her true calling in the world of plumbing supplies. The truth is, I appreciated a well-appointed bathroom as much as the next person. In fact, I appreciated a well-appointed bathroom probably a lot more than the next person. I couldn't help it. I'd grown up thinking about bathrooms. I just didn't want to think about bathrooms as a career.

"Thanks," I said. And then, to be nice: "I'll think about it."

# 7

If you are not an unmarried Jewish woman still living in your hometown, count your non-Jewish blessings. You'll never find yourself in the uncomfortable circumstance of being invited to a family dinner only to find out later that the entire dinner was merely a ploy to set you up with an Orthodox man you would never in a million years have consented to have dinner with, if only you'd known he was going to be there. Which is what happened a few minutes after my dad walked into my sister's house. Suddenly, my brother-in-law was standing in front of me, a strange man to his side.

"Rena," Aryeh said, "I'd like you to meet Chaim."

The room fell silent as everyone turned to watch me meet the man they had all decided was my future husband, a man with a beard and a full head of dark curly hair. Or what appeared to be a full head of dark curly hair—you never know what sort of bald spot might be lurking beneath the skullcap.

I looked at my mother with what I hoped conveyed anger,

disgust, and the implicit threat of never speaking to her again. Certainly, she'd been in on this setup. As if I'd go out with a religious guy! Just how low did they think I'd sunk?

"Nice to meet you," I said. I knew better than to stick out my hand for a handshake. Men don't touch women in the world of the religious, not even women protected by a full round of relatives standing no more than six inches away.

"Nice to meet you, too," Chaim said. "I've heard a lot about you."

I nodded my head at this piece of information, wondering exactly who had told him exactly what. Not that it mattered—it's not like I'd ever be seeing him again. Still, it bothered me that this stranger had any information about me at all when yours truly had been kept completely in the dark about his existence in return.

"Don't believe any of it," I said.

At that, Ron laughed a little too loudly—or maybe it only seemed that way. He was suddenly seriously invading my personal space. In another all-black getup, Ron was looking less and less like a serial killer and more and more like John Travolta all the time. Need I say this fact pretty much threw a zinger into my plans for a John Travolta Weekend anywhere in the near future? He looked at me, and then at Chaim, and then back at me again.

"I think you'll find you two have a lot in common," he said.

I looked at Chaim and wondered what in God's name Ron was talking about. Just because we were both humans, unmarried, and stuck in my sister's house for the evening didn't mean we had a whole heck of a lot in common. Unless Chaim had recently stolen a dog.

"You like animals?" I asked him.

"Excuse me?"

"Oh, nothing. Inside joke."

A minute later, I found Alicia in the kitchen, doing a terrible acting job of pretending everything was perfectly normal. Guests for *Shabbos*! Everybody has guests for *Shabbos*!

"Not in a million years," I said to her.

She blanched.

"It was Aryeh's idea," she said.

"Well, next time, tell him to forget it."

"You don't know," she said. She took a deep breath and blew it out again. "It's hard to say no to Aryeh."

I looked at my sister, and she studiously avoided my gaze.

"Something going on I should know about?"

She shook her head, but in an entirely unconvincing manner.

"What is it?" I asked.

Alicia opened the refrigerator door and poked around.

"I think Chaim's pretty cute," she said.

"You don't want to tell me, that's fine."

Alicia looked quickly around the kitchen, as though we were sneaking a bite of a ham sandwich and she was afraid we'd be caught.

"I'll call you," she said. "Is that okay?"

Of course it was okay. Even though our spiritual lives

have gone in vastly different directions—Alicia's to synagogue and mine to nowheresville—we're still sisters, and we're still there for each other.

"Call me. Come over. Whatever," I said.

Alicia pulled a pitcher of grape juice from the fridge, closed the refrigerator door, and dashed out of the kitchen.

It was time to light the Sabbath candles at the dining room table, something my mother did with a newly acquired flare for the Eastern European dramatic. First she draped her head with a big doily (did she crochet that, too?). Then she waved her hands in front of the lit candles in three great sweeps. Next she covered her face with her palms, leaving her fingers lightly pressed to her forehead. And finally—after taking a moment to compose herself—she recited the prayer in her halting Hebrew.

When she was finished, Ron clapped his hands.

"Well done, Helen!" he said.

My mother pulled the doily from her head and gave Ron one of her beaming smiles. She looked like a third grader, ready to receive a gold Jewish star for proper prayer recitation. Who *was* this person? For as long as I could remember, I'd been wishing my mother would turn from her meddling self into somebody else, but this new crazy-in-love mother of mine wasn't exactly what I'd had in mind.

From beneath the table came a rousing cheer and then a round of knocking noises. I felt a hand clasp my ankle and looked down to see at least three of Alicia's kids on the floor, doing some kind of dance on their knees while pounding on the underside of the table. One of the kids began to slap my father's shins.

"Let go," I said.

"Oh, for Christ's sake," my dad said.

"Al!" my mother said.

"Let's wash!" Aryeh called out.

Oy, the number of rituals you must go through before actual eating occurs! I did my best to participate, but somehow, being led through a litany of religious prayers and rituals by a sister who only a few years before had been my main supplier of weed and various hallucinogens cast a slightly sarcastic pall over the proceedings. I can't help but hold out the ridiculous hope that one day she'll whip off the wig and offer me a joint for old times' sake. But that is never going to happen, at least not in this lifetime. Wait—do Jews believe in reincarnation?

"So, Rena, I hear you're a waitress," Chaim said once we'd finally settled down to dinner. Already the kids had managed to turn the white tablecloth into a purple collage of spilled grape juice on top of which mangled chunks of challah sat like table ornaments.

I nodded.

"She actually did go to college," Alicia said.

Alicia was wearing her shoulder-length brown wig, the one with the long bangs hanging in her eyes—a look that left her looking far sexier than her own hair ever had. In fact, you could say she looked sort of like a prostitute, if you were the sort of person who said such things, which fortunately no one was. Although I considered it.

"There's nothing wrong with being a waitress," I said.

"I didn't say there was anything wrong with being a waitress, Miss Sensitive. I was just bringing up the point that you also went to college, once upon a time. And grad school."

"What did you study?" Chaim asked.

"*Ms.* Sensitive. Speech therapy."

"Chaim's a filmmaker," Alicia said.

"Oh?" I said.

"Well, one day I'd like to make films," he said.

"Film?" my dad said. "Like directing? You know who I like? Oh, what's his name? That guy, the Jewish one, makes those movies, you know, Rena, that one I really like?"

"Dad, I haven't been out to a movie with you in years."

"Oh, come on. You know the one. Oh, for Christ's sake. Helen, what's the guy's name?"

"Spielberg?" my mother tried.

"No, no, not Spielberg. That other guy. Funny. You know."

"Adam Sandler?" I said.

"No! God, I'm losing my mind. Ron, you're a doctor. You think I've got Alzheimer's already? Ha! Ha! Ha!"

"Al," my mother said.

"What? I say something wrong?"

"More chicken, Dad?" Alicia asked.

"Look, I'm in wholesale. I didn't go to medical school, all right?"

"Al, calm down," my mother said.

I looked at Chaim. He didn't seem at all flustered by the conversation. In fact, he seemed perfectly at home. I imagined he probably grew up in a universe very much like the one he'd landed in tonight. He probably had his own slew of sisters who wore big wigs and his own slew of brothers-in-law with beards that hung down their chests. Aryeh made a practice of rolling his up and then sticking a bobby pin through the bottom of it to hold the roll of beard in place. I wonder if they teach that sort of thing in Orthodox religious school. Beard Rolling 101. Well, Chaim must have missed that course. In fact, on closer inspection, his beard wasn't much of a beard at all. More like one of those five-day-growth looks, like you see on hunky guys in magazine advertisements.

"So, what kind of films do you want to make?" I asked him.

"God, what was that guy's name?" Al said.

"Don't think about it and it will come to you," Aryeh said.

"Don't tell him what to do," Alicia said.

"I'm not telling him what to do. I'm just suggesting."

"You don't suggest. You tell."

I wondered what was going on. Alicia and Aryeh never bickered in front of other people. And on the *Shabbos*! Wasn't that breaking a commandment or two?

"Religious films?" I asked Chaim.

"Religious films?"

"Yeah, you know. Jewish stuff."

Chaim laughed. "No. I don't want to make religious films."

"Rena always wanted to be an actress," Alicia said.

"Oh, please," I said.

"You did! And she watches more movies than anybody I know."

"Nobody you know watches movies."

"He's made a million movies," Al said.

"Woody Allen!" my mother said.

"Yes!" my father said. "Oh, thank God. Woody Allen."

"What about him?" I asked.

"Nothing. Nothing. Woody Allen. Wood-y Al-len. That's the one. Thank you, Helen."

"You're welcome, Al."

My parents still love each other, they just can't live together. This small, difficult-to-ignore obstruction to their relationship took twenty-nine years to rectify. My father, after nearly three decades of general moaning about the way my mother ran his life, finally made real on his constant threats to move out. Like magic, this solved everything. Living apart for their trial separation, my parents soon found they had absolutely nothing in common besides their two daughters and a shared Visa bill, and despite their love and affection for each other, there was no sense in continuing. It was an entirely amicable divorce, followed by the unlikely development of a true, albeit strange, friendship between them. Suddenly, they had the patience to listen to each other. My father continued to eat dinner at my mother's house three or four times a week. They took in the occasional movie and even kept on with their monthly couples book group. They didn't fight anymore. Divorce was the best thing that ever happened to their marriage.

At least it was until my mother met Ron.

I finally figured out why the kids were so hyper. There was no television humming away to lull them into a complete hypnotic stupor. It was *Shabbos*, and the electricity couldn't be switched on or off again until the sun set the next evening. The kids had been left with no choice but to find something to do that had no relationship to technology. As the evening wore on, that choice seemed finally to whittle down to a lot of slugging it out with one another on the floor. Fortunately, my dad had fallen asleep on the couch and no longer had to view the action that would have threatened to give him a coronary.

"I better get going," I said.

I had a big night in front of me—a dog to take out, a set of teeth to floss, a couple of Jason Robards movies to watch. Besides, I didn't want Chaim to think I was interested. Best way to nip things in the bud was to take off, pronto.

"So early?" Alicia asked.

"Yeah, sorry. Places to go, things to do, people to see."

My mother looked up from her coffee, whitened with kosher nondairy creamer. "You're leaving?"

"Yeah. Time to get going."

"You can't stay a little bit longer?"

"I'm sorry, I really can't. But we'll have lunch or something. Soon."

This always seemed to work—the promise of a future lunch—despite the fact I almost never came through with such a plan. And yet it always seemed to give my mother the great hope that one day we'd be the best friends she was constantly saying she wanted us to be. Oh, the bright, shining future!

"Oh, that sounds nice!" she said. "Aviva, you'll come, too."

"I wish you didn't have to go," Alicia said to me.

I threw my arms around my sister and gave her a big kiss on the side of her head. Her wig smelled exactly like brisket.

"Sorry, Alicia." I pulled back and looked her in the eye. "Call me, right?"

She nodded.

"Hey," Chaim said. "I've got to get going, too."

Everyone looked at him as he rose from his chair.

"What's going on?" my dad asked, suddenly awake.

"They're leaving," my mother said.

"Leaving?"

"Rena and Chaim. They're leaving."

"Together?"

I patted my dad on the arm. "No, no, Dad. It's just time to go."

"Maybe Rena could give you a ride," Alicia said to Chaim.

"Oh, that's all right. I've got my bike."

"A ride?" I said.

"No, really. I've got my bike. I've got lights and everything. No problem."

"No, I mean, you'd take a ride?"

"Well, if I didn't have my bike. But I do. See? I'm riding." He picked up a bike helmet from the fireplace hearth and shoved it on his head. "Helmet."

He circled the room, thanking Aryeh and my sister for dinner and telling everyone else how nice it had been to meet them. Then we walked out the front door together and down the steps to the sidewalk. I'm pretty sure the entire family was watching from the living room window.

"But I thought you were, you know, religious," I said.

"Me? Religious? I'm not religious."

"You're not?"

"No."

"Okay."

"Okay?"

"Yeah. Sorry. Whatever."

"Why? Are you religious?"

"Me?"

"Yeah, you."

"No. I'm not religious. Look. I'm driving. See? Not religious."

"I didn't really think you were religious."

"Oh."

Chaim shrugged.

I opened the door to my car and sat in the driver's seat,

wondering where Aryeh had managed to dig up Chaim if he wasn't religious. He certainly looked religious. But maybe that was all in the yarmulke. Even Brian had looked pretty much Jewish with a yarmulke on his head. Now that Chaim had removed the religious head adornment and replaced it with a bike helmet, he looked a lot more like just a regular guy with a five-day growth on his chin. There was a knock on the window, and I unrolled it.

"My name's not Chaim," Chaim said.

"It's not?"

"God, no. That's just what Aryeh calls me."

"Oh, because I thought . . ."

"Yeah. I just figured that out. The name and everything. Pretty religious-sounding."

"Yeah."

He placed a foot into one of the bike pedal stirrups, pushed down, and began to bike away down the street.

"Well, what is it, then?" I called after him.

"What?"

"Your name," I called out. "What's your name?"

He turned his head so that I could see his face as he rolled down the street in the distance.

"It's Chuck," he yelled.

# 8

When I first met Brian, I was going out with Phillip Rosen. Dear, sweet Phillip Rosen, whom my parents loved not only because he planned on going to law school after college, and not only because he was an awfully nice guy, and not only because he could talk sports ad nauseam with my father, and not only because he always managed to compliment my mother's cooking and managed to sound sincere while doing it, but also—*mostly,* when it came right down to it—mostly because he turned out to be a Jewish guy. A Jewish guy! They saw ivory wedding invitations in their dreams, embossed with the Star of David. They saw themselves dancing a wild and sweaty hora to the beat of a klezmer band, their daughter, the bride, held aloft on a chair by half-crazed, Manischewitz-filled well-wishers. They saw themselves beaming—the proud grandparents at the bris, the bar or bat mitzvah, the wedding. Such *naches* in their future!

It goes without saying that they weren't too happy when I

broke dear, sweet, Jewish Phillip Rosen's heart, dumping him with little ceremony for the guy he made the mistake of bringing along to dinner one night.

Joke is, I hadn't even been taken with Brian at first. I thought he was a bit of an asshole, really, the way he went on and on down there at the end of the table about some mountain he planned to climb the following summer. A mountain? Who cared? I'd lived my entire life in the Pacific Northwest, surrounded by mountain climbers and skiers and hikers—lovers of the great outdoors who smelled of burning wood, wet wool, and unwashed hair. Adventure seekers: There couldn't be a more boring, self-centered bunch. Forever doing pull-ups and push-ups and shopping at the REI for crampons and freeze-dried food. I had no interest in any of it.

We'd all gone for Mexican food downtown, a group of Phillip's hiking buddies and me, and I cleared my platter, barely listening to the conversation around the table. They were all drinking anyway, and there are few things worse than a drunken group of climbers, with their stories of near death experiences and bouts of diarrhea in the wilderness. When Brian called the next day, I had no idea who he was.

"You met me last night," he said. "Come on. Brian. At the end of the table."

"Oh, *you*," I said.

"Try to put a little bit of excitement in your voice when you say that."

"Look, I'm kind of busy," I said. "What do you want?"

"I thought maybe I could take you to dinner sometime."

"What are you, some kind of asshole friend of Phillip's? Asking his girlfriend out?"

Brian laughed. "Guess so," he said.

He was standing at my apartment door about fifteen minutes later, oozing his brand of notoriously powerful pheromones and smiling with all the blond, bad-boy charm of Brad Pitt in *Thelma & Louise*. I'm ashamed to admit it, but I didn't even hesitate. I let him in.

"God, you really *are* an asshole," I said to him.

"Yeah. But you're the one who opened the door."

"Well, I'm an asshole, too, I guess."

Romantic, no? If only I'd listened to myself way back then.

For the first few years of our relationship, Brian continued to hold out the vain hope that with a little shove in the right direction, I'd finally see the light and find myself as enamored as he was with the great outdoors. To this end, he took me on weekend rock-climbing trips, talked me into getting inside of white-water kayaks, dragged me along on mountain-biking treks. Oh, I tried. I really did. I had lots of seriously uncomfortable sex inside of dank, smelly tents. I went days without showering. I felt the inside of my nose crust up, forgot about getting a brush through my hair, peed behind bushes, searched the sky for shooting stars. Sometimes I even had fun pretending I was someone that I wasn't.

The problem wasn't so much nature itself as Brian's approach to getting close to nature. You couldn't just take a day hike, for example. He'd never consider going for a calm paddle on a still lake or, God forbid, car camping. No, Brian's idea of a good time was more like class-four rapids in the middle of nowhere or doing a first ascent of a climbing route in Patagonia. If there weren't some chance of death or at least great bodily harm in whatever he approached, Brian didn't see the point.

Meanwhile, Phillip Rosen has a wife, three children, and a thriving law practice in Philadelphia.

The Big Guy hadn't budged an inch since I'd left him asleep on the floor several hours earlier, his big body spread across the blankets that used to grace my bed. When I walked into the apartment after coming home from Alicia's that Friday night, his head popped up for only the briefest instant before dropping back down again.

"Come here, Big Guy," I said.

He didn't move.

"Don't you need to go out?"

No interest. One day and already the dog was bored with me.

"Fine," I said to him. "Be that way."

I petted the fur on his back, causing a few thousand dog hairs to separate from their host and flutter to my apartment floor.

"The night is young," I said to him.

I turned on my computer to check e-mails. Maybe Brian had decided to write again and beg me to come back. I hadn't checked my e-mails in four hours. You never knew—those four hours may have been the very same four hours when Brian finally realized the great mistake he'd made and decided to write and tell me all about it.

I opened my in-box. Nothing from Brian. One message from a poetry Web site that sent me a poem every day that I promptly deleted every day without reading; a message from the library that I didn't bother to open because the fact that I have overdue books and an ever-growing fine was simply not news anymore but merely a given; a message from my good friends Horny Gals and another from the darlings at WeBCAm babes; a 10-percent-off coupon from Best Buy; a forward of a forward of a joke from one of the bartenders at Sammy's Place, which was bound to be a really stupid joke I'd already been forwarded at some point in the last six months; a message from Lisa (Subject: "FAVOR!!"), which was a request for Ambien if I had any to spare, which I didn't; and, finally, a demand from my old high school friend Gloria that I go out for drinks with the old high school posse one night next week.

I needed a new class of friends, preferably of the type who wrote witty e-mails. I spent the next little while looking at old messages from Brian and forcing myself to delete them one by one. When finally I went to my trash bin to empty it, my trash bin tried to talk me out of it.

"Are you sure you want to permanently delete all of the messages in this folder?" it asked me.

"No," I said, but then I hit the delete button and sent everything away forever.

Now there was only the shoebox of cards and letters to

contend with, the seven years' worth of written correspondence from Brian that I'd saved, already planning for that elderly future when surely I'd be poking through the attic in search of the love letters of my youth. The only snag in the plan was that Brian couldn't write a decent love letter to save his life. Nor was he prolific in his output. In ten years, I'd collected six Hallmark birthday cards, eleven short letters (written by kerosene lamp at various campsites), several postcards, a napkin on which he'd drawn a heart with our names nestled safely within its borders, a pack of matches with the words *Let's fuck* written on the inside, and one naked drawing he'd done of me late one night while stoned out of his mind. That was it. The total written accumulation of our relationship, Brian to Rena. Meanwhile, somewhere hidden deep in his closet or perhaps now safely packed away in his parents' garage, lies the other half of the correspondence—the Rena to Brian half, the dozens of letters I'd spilled out in manic happiness or fretful anguish. The cards I'd made by hand to amuse him, with cutout photos and snippets from magazines. The stupidly funny poems, short love notes, long, crazy love letters. Take that, elderly Brian! Take that, old man, sifting through the cards and letters of your youth, seeing—far too late—that this woman loved you like none before or since! I spit on you, you poor, pitiful, ancient, balding, potbellied, impotent Brian! You who sees only now the huge error of your ways!

And yet, I was nearly positive he'd never look at my letters again. In fact, he'd probably dumped the whole load the moment he moved from his apartment into the house he now shared with Anna—a thought that prompted me, in that moment, to do the same.

Then I sat on the sofa, waiting for inspiration. I no longer felt like watching the Jason Robards movies. When you're alone and depressed, it's a good idea to pass on *Magnolia* and *Philadelphia* unless you've already made a firm commitment to kill yourself. Finally, I decided to paint my fingernails, and before I had the chance to change my mind, I shoved myself forward to the bathroom to hunt down a bottle of fingernail polish.

Ah, my lovely bathroom! In an apartment that otherwise seriously lacks in the feng shui department, my bathroom is testament to the beauty of direct access to plumbing supplies. Not for Al's daughter the leaky, dated, mildew-infested, and hopelessly stained fixtures that for years prior had occupied the water closet. With Carl's tacit approval, I'd transformed all of it—from toilet to tiles to shower door—into a charming yet eclectic design of my own making. I'd found a lovely marble-topped side table at a garage sale that I'd had fitted with a new white porcelain sink, replaced the toilet with a modern design that used gallons less water to operate, and mixed and matched brushed nickel hardware from various catalogs in my father's shop for a look that blended together without being boring. I'd tiled the entire shower myself with sage-colored subway tile and bought a beautiful gilded mirror for practically nothing from a shop in Georgetown that specializes in reclaimed household items. You could say I was inordinately proud of the transformation, and you'd be right. Too bad being proud of one's bathroom isn't exactly cause for public adoration.

Of course, charm doesn't automatically translate into clean and organized. After fishing through drawers filled with half-empty containers of old creams, lotions, shampoos, gels, and other varieties of smelly, dripping gunk, as well as a generous supply of beat-up odds and ends (dull razors, wrapped soaps, used lipsticks, odd pills, rusted barrettes, dried-up mascaras, and on and on), I finally netted one ancient purple bottle of nail polish, only to find it wouldn't open. Oh, the frustration! So close and yet so far away from finally accomplishing something productive, shallow and inconsequential as it may have been. I knocked the bottle's rim against the bathroom vanity a few times, ran hot water over the lid, dried it off completely with a towel, and eventually managed to yank off the top, by which time I'd decided to paint my toenails instead. And after that, it became crystal clear that my eyebrows were in desperate need of some serious plucking—a task I took to with far more gusto than the job deserved. Then I had to hunt through the bathroom drawers again until I located an eyebrow pencil to darken the spots you could see through thanks to my overzealous plucking. It seemed a good idea about then to get out of the bathroom before I started examining my face for what would surely turn into an evening of regrettable home surgical operations, so I ended up back on the sofa where I'd started out an hour and a half before.

I picked up an ancient women's magazine I'd bought at

the library book sale for a dime and leafed through it, knowing I'd find nothing worth reading but giving each page a serious looking-over anyway, seeing as how I had nothing else to occupy me if I came to the last page too soon. Tucked between an article on cheating spouses and how to get the most out of your European spa vacation was a short, zippy piece called "Steps to a More Connected Life." A more connected life. I could use more connections now that my key connection had been severed for good. I ran my finger down the column of suggestions:

1. Try throwing a dinner party or two!
2. Take a class of some kind—yoga, maybe. Or cooking.
3. Join a group or a club.
4. Volunteer.
5. Exercise!
6. Get a dog.

What do you know? One down, five to go.

"Hey, you," I said to the Big Guy.

He didn't move.

"Hey," I said.

The Big Guy opened one eye halfway and stared at me.

"Come here."

He shut his eye.

"Really. Come here."

Nothing. I stood up, grabbed the leash, and held it in front of me.

"Let's go out. Come on, boy. Let's go. Seriously. Come on, now."

Still nothing.

"Here we go, Big Guy. Here we go."

I couldn't even connect with a dog. Things were not boding well for my future with a human.

"Fine," I said. "Be that way."

I plunked down onto the floor next to him and scratched his belly. He wasn't the best company in the world, but then again, he wasn't the worst, either.

"*Philadelphia* or *Magnolia*?" I asked him.

# 9

My love life, abridged edition:

When I was thirteen, Matt Stone dumped me for Linda Acres, she of the great legs. I didn't even know women had such a thing as great legs back then, but Matt Stone did. Suddenly, our long afternoons of making out on the single bed in his basement bedroom under a smelly army blanket were over. He hardly glanced at me in the hallways of Captain Charles Wilkes Junior High after that. You'd have thought he'd never in his life tried to shove his hand up the front of my shirt and then, finding the route impassable, tried shoving his hand down my pants instead. You'd have thought he'd never looked at me with his huge brown eyes and long eyelashes like a girl's and told me that he really, really liked me. But I couldn't have cared less. Making out with him hadn't been all that much fun anyway. I hadn't yet equated "boyfriend" with a person you wanted to be with. I thought it was all about making out.

Then, the summer before ninth grade, I fell hard for Daniel Berenbach at a camp for Jewish teens. Suddenly, I knew what love was. Love was Daniel Berenbach's sun-kissed face and skinny golden chest. Love was Daniel Berenbach choosing to sit next to me at the Saturday night campfire. Love was Daniel Berenbach sneaking out of his cabin after lights out to stand under the window of my cabin and make the ridiculous cooing noises that were my cue to sneak out, too. Love was letting Daniel Berenbach shove his hand up my shirt under the pine trees at the foot of Lake Tanwax, while the stars I'd never noticed before filled the black sky. Love was the heartbreak of leaving Daniel Berenbach on the last day of camp and pledging to somehow see him again, even though he lived in San Francisco and I lived in Seattle. And love was finding out that love can end on a dime, as happened to me four months later when I ended up in San Francisco on a family trip to visit ancient relatives only to find out that the boy I once loved no longer had a suntan or a head of long, tousled hair. He was just a boy in a pair of green pants. Goodbye, Daniel Berenbach!

Tenth grade was one long bad-hair year for me, along with a few bouts of embarrassing acne, but I made up for it in the eleventh grade by falling in love with Neil Matthews and having sex with him after five months of his interminable begging. This was before condoms were handed out as door prizes at high school parties, back when you had to actually go into a drugstore and ask to purchase them, which Neil

Matthews bravely did at a drugstore nowhere near Lincoln High School.

"Yes, I'm looking for prophylactics," Neil said to the pharmacist—the repeated recitation of which later, as we sat naked in his parents' bed while they were out for the evening, sent me into a state of hysterical laughter horribly exacerbated a moment later by the sight of Neil's erect penis. Up until that moment, I'd never really seen one, only felt one pressed hard against my leg or cupped in my hand in the darkness of Neil's parents' sedan. But here it was, long and hard, wrapped in a rubber, and fumbling its way toward the entrance to my tense, petrified vagina. Somehow, we persevered. We were teenagers, after all. But the experience put me off of sex for a good five more months, by which time Neil Matthews had left me for the far more experienced, far less hysterical, not to mention seriously well-endowed Tina Phillips.

By senior year, I'd figured out how the whole process was supposed to work. Truth was, you really didn't have to do much. The boy already had a pretty strong sense of direction and hardly needed coaxing. The pangs of male performance anxiety, the dread over penis size, the thought of his partner's enjoyment—all of that was still in the future, as was my knowledge of same. I spent my entire senior year having sex with Gene Muldoon, never realizing that his penis was unusually small. Thank God I found out my freshman year of college. I was beginning to wonder what the big deal about sex was all about. Turned out Gene Muldoon, along with being poorly endowed, had also been poorly equipped in the technique department. It took Billy St. Clair to show me the errors of Gene Muldoon's ways, followed by several others—the number of which I am not inclined to reveal—and ending with Phillip Rosen. Suffice it to say that by the time I met Brian, I pretty well knew my way around the block. Then, seven years of Brian.

And now, nobody.

I woke Saturday morning to a phone message from my mother, wondering what I'd thought of the single Jewish guy Alicia had snuck on me the night before. Of course, she didn't call him the "single Jewish guy." She called him the "very nice boy." But first she droned on about Alicia's cooking and Ronald's yarmulke. Finally, she got down to the point of her phone call.

"And didn't that Chaim seem like a very nice boy?" she said to my voice mail. Silence. Then: "Okay . . . call me!"

If it weren't for the fact that it was still the Jewish Sabbath until sundown—no telephone day for the Orthodox—I'm quite sure Alicia would have called to leave the same message.

Alicia. I made a mental note to remember to call my sister. Or maybe I needed to wait until she called me. If she'd had a fight with Aryeh, it could very easily have blown over by now—maybe she was even hoping I'd forgotten all about it so that she didn't have to explain the whole thing. Didn't all couples fight every once in a while? If my sister needed to call me, she'd call me.

I took the Big Guy out, returned him to my apartment, ran out to buy a coffee, and then, despite my better judgment, called my mother back. Better to get the conversation over with than to deal with the series of voice mails that otherwise awaited me.

"Yes, I'm sure he's very nice, Ma," I told her. "But then, who knows? He could be a serial killer."

"He's not a serial killer."

"How do you know?"

"He's not a serial killer. I know."

"You never know."

"Stop it," my mother said.

"Stop what?"

"You know stop what. He was very nice."

"I don't need setting up."

"Fine. We won't set you up, then."

"Good."

"Because you're doing very well on your own."

"Thank you," I said.

"I was being sarcastic," my mother said.

"You're kidding."

My mother sighed. "But he did seem nice, didn't he?" she said.

Conversations with my mother are always exhausting.

Even though I wasn't thrilled by my family's attempt to set me up with Chuck/Chaim, the truth was that I wouldn't have minded meeting a guy. But how did a person meet guys, anyway? I was seriously out of practice. Before—when Brian was still my boyfriend—meeting guys seemed the easiest thing in the world. They were everywhere. Eyeing me from across a bar, or asking to share my table at a crowded coffee shop, or making conversation with me in line at the grocery store. But inevitably, I suppose, in the exact same second I suddenly truly needed the attention, the entire cadre of available men simply disappeared. Oh, I suppose men *would* have still eyed me from across a bar if I had any intentions of sitting in a bar where men might be able to eye me. But suddenly, the idea of sitting in a bar, or a coffee shop, or making conversation with the man behind me in line at the grocery store, seemed the pinnacle of obvious desperation.

And I certainly wasn't going to go trolling the Internet for dates. All of those humiliating matching-up-people sites with their embarrassing airbrushed photographs and even more embarrassing bios. What could be more exhausting than meeting a guy online and telling him my entire life story, and reading his entire life story in return, only to find—upon meeting in the flesh—that neither of us lived up to the other's expectation? And then the thought of starting the whole rigmarole over yet again! Forget it.

This, I suddenly realized, is why people have dogs.

All evening, the dinner specials at Sammy's Place eluded me. Everything sounded alike. Sauces and spices and herb-crusted whatevers. Why did I have to tell patrons the specials any-way? Couldn't they just read them like they read the rest of the menu? And why did we have to attempt to make the specials sound so especially appealing? Wasn't that just an-other way of pointing out that the other menu items were *not* special? The whole thing seemed like a very poor business tactic.

Lisa, meanwhile, was having no problem remembering the specials. I saw her across the restaurant in her section, smiling and chatting and acting as though she would rather be nowhere else than serving huge, unhealthy platters of food to her half-baked customers. Her hair sat on her head in its usual monstrous, twisted, falling-out bun, a style that makes most women look sexy, but which only makes Lisa look like she needs a new pair of glasses to see what she's doing. De-spite her happy demeanor, I knew all of the smiling and chit-chat and ability to focus on the specials was only an act—she'd taken a hit of Adderall at the start of her shift, and her mind wouldn't be shutting down for hours.

Sammy's Place is what my father would call a "throw-back." With its swanky red booths, dim lighting, and ob-scenely large bar drinks, it attracts patrons from all points on the hip spectrum. The young, the old, the very hungry, those looking only for a touch of solid to accompany their heavy load of liquid nutrition, and those who come for the gigantic portions of good old-fashioned meat—they all head to Sam-my's Place. I'd say about three-fourths of the clientele were regulars, and of those a good three-fourths were men with very bad pickup lines. You'd be surprised how many guys enjoy being told to fuck off by a woman in a waitress uniform.

Of course, there were the nice regulars, too, like Steve with the ponytail, who drove a taxi during the three hours a week he wasn't hanging out at Sammy's; or Marty in the leather jacket, who sat all day in one of the booths, pulling papers out of an old briefcase and typing away on a laptop; or eightyish Paul, with the gold watch and the greasy comb-over, who came in three or four nights a week, called me "Beautiful" like some kind of horny grandfather, and winked a lot.

One day, I told myself, I will no longer be a waitress. I'll no longer live in the same apartment I've lived in since college, or even in the same city where I've always lived. I'll have a career, a real career that's meaningful and interesting. One that makes me feel worthwhile. And I'll have a great boyfriend, a boyfriend who won't dump me for a new athletic, outdoorsy girlfriend. No, he'll love *me,* the real deep-down me, even though the real deep-down me is frankly not all that deep. He will understand how I could do something so stupid as to steal my old boyfriend's new girlfriend's dog. "Well, duh!" he will say. "Of course you stole it!" He will find my occasional bouts with acne amusing and youthfully attractive. He will want nothing more than to have sex with me on those occasions when he will miraculously know that I want to have sex, even though I am sending out no signals whatsoever that such a thing is on my mind. And when I don't want to have sex, he will know that, too. He will be exactly like Brian without being Brian. He will be the Brian who would have never left me.

But in the meantime, I needed the tips.

# 10

Mornings were for sleeping. Evenings were for working at Sammy's Place. It was the in-between hours that sometimes threw me for a loop. But that Sunday—home on the couch with a sleeping Big Guy by my side, a Diet Coke, a package of Red Vines, and *The Big Easy* on TNT—I had pretty much under control. I was just on the verge of summoning up the energy to get online and add a few Dennis Quaid movies to my rental queue when the phone rang. Alicia. So she did want to talk.

"Hey."

But it wasn't my sister. It was Brian.

"Brian?"

"Yeah. What are you doing?"

Of the thousands of possible responses, I somehow decided on the truth.

"Well, let's see," I said to him. "Drinking Diet Coke. Watching a movie. Eating Red Vines."

I didn't mention the Big Guy, lying on the couch next to me, asleep.

"Very productive."

"You called to give me shit?"

"No, no. Sorry."

No one said anything for a moment. I looked out the window at the claustrophobic curtain of gray sky, and right then something inside of my head ticked very loudly, making me wonder if I was dying, like maybe the audible tick is what a person hears right before a deadly stroke, only no one who'd heard it before had come back from the dead to let the rest of us know. And then I thought of what a great movie scene that would make—the old boyfriend calling and the woman who loves him gripping the receiver and falling dead from a stroke. And then, of course, I had to say a quick prayer and knock on the wood of the windowsill to make sure I'd stay alive forever, or at least long enough to find out why Brian was calling. Still no one said anything. My head kept ticking. It occurred to me I should have had a contingency plan in place for this exact scenario. Something besides imagining myself dying. I should have had a clever and sarcastic comment prepared, or come to a firm decision that if Brian called, the only sane response would be to slam down the phone, or I should have figured out, well, something. But—no big surprise—I didn't have a plan. Instead I only waited for one of us to say the next thing while my head ticked on ominously. After a moment, it seemed that that somebody was going to have to be me.

"Well, *you* called *me,*" I said.

"Yeah, I did. . . . I was hoping . . . well . . . Look, would you consider meeting me for coffee?"

I didn't answer.

"Yes?" Brian said.

I hadn't spoken to Brian since our last phone call—the one where he told me things were over between us. It didn't seem right that he should call and I should immediately jump. But it was Brian. And I was curious. And also, I was hungry. And on top of it all, the tick in my head was getting in the way of any real thinking. The Big Guy slept next to me, oblivious to everything.

"If food is part of the deal and you're paying for it, then I'll consider it."

"Sure. That'd be great."

"Okay, when?"

"How about now?"

"Now?"

"Yeah. Look down."

I moved my eyes down from the blank sky in front of me to the street below. There stood good old Brian, the man who had ruined my life, waving at me from the sidewalk.

"I'll be right up," he said.

"No!" I said.

At the sound of my yell, the Big Guy sat up on the couch. I shoved him back down before Brian could get a glimpse.

"Somebody up there with you?" Brian said.

"What? Oh. No. Nobody here. I'm alone. I'll be right down."

"Okay," Brian said. "Okay, that'd be great."

It was much less weird to see Brian in person than I had imagined. In fact, it seemed downright normal except for the fact that I felt like shoving a fork into his forehead. Although I don't think Brian found it so normal. He gave me an awkward kiss on the cheek like I was some long-lost cousin of his and not the woman he used to supposedly love. Then he stepped back and gave me one of his smiles, and I swear, my insides did a somersault. Brian can do that to a girl. Or two.

"You look good," he said.

I rolled my eyes at him. "Don't say stupid things," I said.

He nodded.

"Unless you want to," I said. "I mean, if you really want to elaborate on how good I look, feel free."

"You look very good. Very, very good. You look great."

"Now you're getting carried away."

We walked down the street, and I let him struggle to find something to chitchat about—the weather, my parents, his parents, the weather again, my sister, his brother—until we ended up at the place where we always went. Always used to go. The Greek place on Madison. It escapes me now why this restaurant, of all places, should have been our favorite. It wasn't as though the food were any good, although it was passable. And we certainly didn't go for the ambience. There was no attempt, for instance, to mask the fact that the restaurant is simply one big, plain rectangular room with a bunch of tables and chairs plunked down inside of it. Sure, a few Greek decorations had been hauled in at some point—plaster statues of nearly naked people posed on white plaster columns; paintings of someone's idea of the Grecian countryside; a stencil, running along the wall near the ceiling, of purple grape clusters and green vines. But none of it worked. Overall the place lacked character, which is probably why, come to think of it, we liked it. Sometimes the absence of attitude can be very refreshing.

Brian was wearing the same old clothes he always did, a fact I found surprisingly disappointing. I guess I'd been hoping that he'd need a total makeover to get me out of his system. That the new woman in his life would insist he change his hair, or get a new jacket, or quit wearing black shoes with white socks and jeans. But there he was, the same Brian I'd always known, who didn't need to reinvent himself, only his girlfriend. The only change was his nervousness around me, something that became even more apparent when we were sitting across from each other at the Greek place, waiting for our food to arrive. Suddenly, I noticed a tiny quiver in his chin.

"Is your chin quivering?" I asked.

He looked down, then back up at me again.

"Yeah," he said. "I guess I'm a little bit nervous."

"You're kidding."

"No."

"I make you nervous?"

Brian swiped at his chin with his thumb and smiled. "Yeah," he said. "You do."

This was a new one. But then, his departure had been a new one, too. Maybe I was just going to have to get used to a lot of new ones in the future when it came to Brian. Still, I didn't know what to make of his nervousness. Was it a good sign? Was he about to throw himself at my feet and beg for forgiveness? Or did I have it all wrong? Maybe he was only afraid of my reaction once he hit me up with the bone-chilling news that he was marrying his new girlfriend. Now I was nervous.

Our waitress, who looked like a thirteen-year-old playing dress-up in her black miniskirt and black eyeliner and the huge dangly earrings that hung from her pink earlobes, dropped our plates of food in front of us as though she'd been disgusted to have to carry them out to us in the first place.

"Enjoy!" she said in a little chirpy voice before dashing off.

"Do you mind if I ask you a question?" I said.

"Go ahead."

"Why do I make you nervous?"

"I don't know," Brian said. "You just do. Or this does. Seeing you. After everything."

"Speaking of which."

"Yeah. Fucked up, I know. I'm sorry. I told you already I'm sorry, but I'll say it again. It wasn't a good move—the way you found out, and I apologize and I should have handled things better than I did and, well, I'm sorry, that's all. I'm sorry if I hurt you."

*" 'If?' "*

"Yeah. Right. Okay. Sorry."

His chin quivered some more. I decided to bite the bullet.

"You're not getting married, are you?" I asked.

Brian laughed. "No," he said. "Not getting married."

"Right," I said.

"Just . . . nervous."

It was almost endearing, his little chin quiver. I hadn't known about this power I had over Brian. Suddenly, I felt like a Mafia guy who's just brought the traitor to his knees before inflicting the fatal blow. Only I didn't have any blows to give. If only I'd slept with someone else. Derrick, maybe. But I had no ammunition at all.

"So, how are you?" Brian asked.

"Don't ask me that," I said.

"That's a bad question? How are you?"

"Well, how do you think I am?" I asked.

"I didn't mean anything by it. I was just asking. You know. Conversationally."

"Okay. Well, then. I'm great."

"Great?"

"Is that a question?"

"No, no. It's great that you're great. That's all."

Brian looked at his plate. His hamburger sat untouched, perched like royalty on its frilly lettuce throne, guarded by two black olives and one long pickle spear. The teenage-looking waitress appeared again to fill our already full water glasses.

"Everything okay?" she asked in her chirping soprano.

"Fine, fine," Brian said. "Great."

She flittered away to fill the water glasses at the next table. The place was chock-full, mostly with college students and couples with small children. No one seemed to have teenagers, only babies and toddlers, little screaming things crushing crackers or spilling drinks while their parents continued talking to each other. A baby let out a wail a few tables away and we both automatically turned toward the sound. The mother picked a pacifier off the floor and popped it back into the baby's mouth.

I'd ordered the Greek salad, which turned out to be iceberg lettuce with a single tomato wedge and a few kalamata olives. I cut the tomato into six pieces and then moved them around my plate. I wasn't hungry anymore. I sat up straighter in my chair.

"So. What's new?" I asked.

"What's new?"

"Well, besides the obvious."

"Nothing, really."

"Still selling fleece?"

"Still selling fleece."

"Okay, then. All caught up."

I laughed my stupid laugh, the one that falls out of my mouth when nothing is funny. Seeing Brian had definitely been a mistake. Too many old feelings were rushing to the surface, like a bad case of hives. I didn't want to love the guy anymore, but it seemed I didn't have a choice in the matter. Brian smiled at me.

"Get this," he said. "Some asshole stole our dog."

My face froze up in its laughing position and wouldn't release. I could feel the word *guilty* emerging in gorged veins across my forehead.

"You're kidding."

"I'm not."

"You have a dog?"

"Well, it's Anna's, really. But, you know. Sort of both of ours."

"Wow. A dog. You and Anna have a dog."

"Had a dog. Somebody stole it. Right out of its run in the backyard."

"I can't believe it."

"Can't believe I have a dog or that someone stole it?"

I shook my head. "Both, I guess," I said.

"Man, Anna's ready to have a breakdown. She's crazy about that stupid dog."

I nodded. Then I shook my head. Then I nodded again. I didn't know what I was doing or what I should say. Was it bad that Anna was ready to have a breakdown? Should I have been feeling sorry for her? And why did he call the Big Guy a "stupid dog"? Didn't he like the stupid dog? Any moment now, I was going to 'fess up to the whole thing and just let Brian call the cops.

"That really sucks," I said. "Who would do such a thing?"

"I don't know."

"Wow. Stealing a dog. That's low. Low. Low. Low. Super-low. The lowest. Lower than low."

"I know."

"Wow. Go figure. Of all the dogs. Yours. You don't think the dog just ran away?"

"Nah. Whoever it was left the gate wide open. Stolen. Definitely."

I nodded. I wondered how in the world to change the subject. I hoped my face wasn't turning as red as it felt. I stared deeply into my salad as though searching for the perfect spot to land my fork. My mind was utterly empty of any subject but the yellow lab in my apartment.

"This is terrible to say," Brian said, "but the truth is, I'm kind of glad that dog's gone."

I stabbed at a wedge of lettuce. "Oh?"

"I don't like animals. Not as pets, anyway. You know that."

"I know that."

"So it's kind of a lucky deal to have the dog go missing. God, that sounds so awful. But I'm just being honest."

"That's you! Mr. Honesty!"

"I tried to act, you know, sad and everything. I know, it's terrible. But really. What dumb luck!"

I looked at Brian. Was it possible he was fooling with me? Had Derrick called and reported my thievery? Did Brian know the Big Guy was, at that moment, most likely taking a dump in the middle of my living room?

Brian laughed. I laughed. Brian laughed harder. He picked up his hamburger and took a big, clownish bite. I laughed as though I'd never seen anything so goddamned funny in my entire life. I picked up a kalamata olive and tossed it at Brian.

"Yeah!" I spat out through my laughter. "Lucky you!"

Brian stuck the olive in his mouth. "God, it's really good to see you again," he said.

My laughter calmed slowly and then finally came to a stop.

"So, is that why you wanted to see me? To tell me about your dog? What's the dog's name again?"

"Tilly."

"Tilly?"

"Yeah. Tilly."

I nodded, as though this piece of information were both new and incredibly interesting.

"Bad name," I said.

"Anna named him."

I nodded.

"I just wanted to see you," he said.

My nodding continued.

"I don't know. I missed you, I guess," he said.

I'd become my own bobble-head doll. Nod, nod, nod.

"I mean, we spent a long time together and everything."

Major nod action.

"And it just seems weird to, you know, cut things off so abruptly. I mean, we're adults, right? We can be friends, right?"

I was starting to get dizzy from all the nodding. I decided to change tactics and began to shake my head.

"No?"

"God, Brian. Be friends?"

"Yeah? Maybe? Is that such a bad idea?"

"I don't want to be your friend."

"You don't?"

"No. I don't."

Now it was Brian's turn to nod.

"Why would I want to be friends with you? What do I get out of it?"

Brian nodded as though he totally understood.

"Look, I have to go," I said.

Brian nodded again.

"Maybe later. Maybe in another lifetime or something we can be big buds," I said.

I stood up to leave.

"Don't go," Brian said.

"Brian, come on."

"Look. Is it okay if I come by sometime? Pick up my things?"

In that moment, it gave me great pleasure to know the only thing of his he'd find at my place would be his new girlfriend's dog. I decided to ignore the question.

"Let me ask you something," I said.

"All right," Brian said.

"Why did you leave me, anyway? What was it? Was I not good-looking enough? Was I too clingy? Did you get tired of me? What?"

Brian looked at me for a moment without saying anything. I could feel his brain cells arguing with one another over how exactly to respond.

"Rena," he said.

"What?" I said. "What was it? Just tell me."

"You're a great woman. You are. And I love you. You're like, the best."

I nodded. Brian didn't say anything else.

"That's it?" I asked him. "I'm the best, so you had to leave me?"

Brian took a breath. "Look," he said. "We're so different, is all. I just didn't think it would work. For the long haul."

I smiled as best I could. "Right," I said.

"I think you're great."

"It's okay."

"I think you've got tons of, you know, potential."

"Potential?"

"It's not coming out right."

"Don't worry about it."

"Rena."

"It's okay."

I backed up a couple of steps.

"Really," I said. "Really, really. No problem. Thanks. Yeah. Right. Oh, I forgot to say. Your stuff? I don't have it anymore. I took it all to the dump. Yeah. Well. Sorry about that. Okay, then. Well, see you. And hey, good luck with that dog thing."

# 11

I've never been much of a pet owner. I once had two gerbils that I kept in a cage in my bedroom and never looked at. They scared me with their little gerbil teeth and nails and their bright black gerbil eyes. At night, they made a lot of noise, digging through wood chips and chewing on cardboard toilet paper rolls and racing on their squeaking wheel, taking manic travels to nowhere. Tell me: What's worse than a couple of unwanted rodents in a cage, making it clear even to the mind of an eleven-year-old the stark aloneness of existence, the prison in which we all must live and eventually die? My dad should have brought home a kitty instead.

I had the gerbils two weeks before I went off to summer camp. I left them in Alicia's care. Secretly, I hoped they'd kick the bucket while I was gone and that Alicia would give them a proper gerbil funeral and sell the cage. But when I came back, there they were, still digging, chewing, and running.

Then a funny thing happened. They died. I'd gone to bed

and suddenly realized that the room was deathly quiet. I turned on the light. There they lay, Ethel and Lucy, dead in a little heap in the corner. Confession: I had more or less forgotten to feed them since coming home from summer camp.

Years later, Alicia made her own confession. I hadn't killed Ethel and Lucy. She had—while I was away. The pair I'd managed to murder were a brand-new pair that Alicia had gone out and purchased in hopes I wouldn't notice. As it turned out, together we'd managed to kill four gerbils. And that was it for pet ownership, until the Big Guy came along.

When Alicia still hadn't called by that afternoon, I decided to take the bull by the horns and call her myself. I have to admit, I was curious. In all the years she'd been married, she'd never had a single negative word to say about her husband. Of course, that could have just been another one of the Orthodox rules I wasn't aware of—not speaking poorly of people behind their backs or something like that. Good rule, actually. Too bad I had no intention of following it.

My sister wasn't home.

"I'll tell her you called," Aryeh told me.

"What time do you expect her back?" I asked.

"I'm really not sure. She didn't say where she was going. But by dinner, anyway. I'll tell her you called, okay?"

I wondered if my sister always took off without mentioning her destination to Aryeh or if this had something to do with whatever had been bothering her on Friday night. And then I wondered where my sister had gone off to.

"Tell her to call me back," I said. "Tell her it's important."

I was trying on all the pants in my closet, looking for a pair that fit or, barring that, a pair that I could actually wear in public without too much embarrassment, when Alicia walked through my door.

"You're here!" I said.

"I'm here."

"I just called you. Like ten minutes ago. Aryeh didn't know where you were."

"Nice pants," she said.

The pair of green straight-legs I'd managed to pull up over my hips were splayed open at the zipper, giving my sister a lovely view of my belly, bulging above the tattered elastic band of my underwear.

"Don't mind me," I said as I yanked at the pant legs and wriggled my thighs.

Alicia sighed, shoved a few rejected pairs of pants off the sofa, and sat down. Despite the fact that she seemed to be on edge, she looked better than usual. Her wig, short and curly, wasn't so awful—she'd played with the bangs enough to make them look almost real. I sat on the floor and stuck my feet in my sister's lap.

"Pull," I said, and she yanked the green pants free of my legs.

"Good thing I showed up," she said.

She stared at the Big Guy for a second. I could feel his presence slowly come into her focus.

"You got a dog?" she asked.

"Pretty much."

"That's nice," she said. "Oh, the super asked me if I was feeling better. Did you tell him I was sick or something?"

"He's just weird," I said.

"And he asked me if I'd come for the dog."

"He did?"

"Yeah."

"Hmm. Weird."

"You're not giving me that dog as a present, are you? Because I seriously do not want a dog."

"No, no, no. You want a Diet Coke?"

"No, thanks."

"How about some crackers?"

I knew she couldn't possibly eat any of my nonkosher crackers even if I had some, which I didn't, but I offered them anyway because I knew she'd say no. Honestly, I've never understood how she manages to continue to keep kosher. I've attempted to understand the concept—how keeping kosher raises the mundane to the sublime, how it makes a person pay attention to the spiritual side of everyday wants and needs—but I still can't get a handle on it. Couldn't a person be thankful each time they ate anything, kosher or not? And once you take on such a commitment—eating special foods and saying certain prayers through thick and through thin—doesn't it immediately take away the spiritual component you were trying to inject in the first place? Aren't you simply reducing it back to the routine, the mundane? But then again, who am I to argue? Thousands of people follow rituals and routines and spiritual paths every day, and if it works for them, that's just hunky-dory.

"No," she said to my cracker offer. "No, thanks."

She glanced around my apartment while I pulled on a pair of sweatpants.

"So what's going on?" I asked her.

She shrugged. "I don't know," she said.

She sighed, and I didn't press the matter. She'd tell me if she wanted to tell me. In the meantime, it was nice having her come by for one of her rare visits. In fact, I couldn't remember the last time she'd stopped by. I sat next to her on the sofa and tried to find something to say.

"You look good today," I said.

"I do?"

"Yeah. You get a new wig or something?"

"New wig?"

"Yeah. It looks good, this one. Very good. Very real."

"Well, it *is* real."

"I know."

All of Alicia's wigs are made of human hair. Very expensive, she's told me. But worth every penny.

"No. You don't know."

"Yes, I do. It's real hair. I know," I said.

"No. This one is *my* real hair."

"You had a wig made out of your hair?"

Alicia looked at me like I was an idiot. Then she reached up and tugged at the hair on her head.

"I mean it's mine. My hair. Attached to my head."

"You're not wearing a *wig*?"

Alicia shook her head. I felt something coil in my gut. This couldn't possibly be good.

"What happened?" I asked.

"I don't know. I got . . . tired of it. I needed a break."

She may as well have told me she'd decided to become a Mormon or have a sex-change operation. It was that surprising.

"Wow," I said.

She nodded.

"Are you . . . you know . . . allowed?"

"What do you mean, 'allowed'?"

"I don't know. Like isn't there a big rule or something?"

She shrugged. "Yeah. Well, no. Well, sort of."

The topic seemed to have exhausted my sister. She leaned against the back of the sofa and shut her eyes.

"I still don't get it," I said after a moment. "I mean, if you don't want to talk about it, that's fine. But what did you mean about needing a break? A break from what? The wig? A break from Aryeh? What?"

She shrugged again, and then her shoulders were shaking and she'd started to weep.

"Hold on," I said.

I went into the bathroom and tore off a wad of toilet paper. Then I brought it to my sister.

"Thanks," she said.

She dabbed at her eyes. The Big Guy, asleep on the floor, took a large breath and let it out again.

"Well," she said, still crying, "I was never too crazy about the wig thing, you know? I mean, of course I understand the point of it and all. I get why Aryeh wants me to wear it. . . ."

I nodded and waited for her to continue. The point of the wig, as far as I'd been told, is in keeping with what many Orthodox Jews consider the laws of modesty. There are plenty of Orthodox Jews who don't go that far, who cover their heads only in synagogue, and then only with a scarf. Or they don't cover their heads at all. But for the very religious Jews, the sight of your real hair is only for your husband. In the meantime, you wear a wig in public so that you still look normal. Or pretty. But not too pretty. Or something like that.

I'd never known that Alicia hadn't been too keen on wearing one.

"I said I'd wear it when I married Aryeh. I thought I could do it. For him. I thought it wasn't too much to ask of me. Because he wanted me to do it. You see? I cover my hair for him. And I don't want to do it anymore. I just don't."

This was news to me, too. I'd had no idea my sister covered her head for her husband and not for herself. She hadn't told me this bit of information before, and it hadn't occurred to me to ask. Chalk it up to those parts of our lives we'd stopped sharing once Alicia became religious, parts that included my own doubts about God as well as any discussion of Brian and his (now former) status as my non-Jewish boyfriend. It makes me sad—the walls we've erected between us—but I've grown to accept our friendship's limitations. More or less. The truth is, I still miss my former sister, the one I grew up with, the one whose life I understood. And so, in that moment, as awful as it was to see her in such a miserable state, I couldn't help but feel happy that she'd come to me.

"Do you need more tissue?" I asked her.

Alicia blew her nose into what was left of the damp wad of toilet paper I'd given her. "Yes, please."

I found a spare roll of toilet paper in the basket I kept beneath my bathroom sink and brought it to her.

"Thanks," she said.

I sat down again and patted my sister's leg.

"The thing is, Aryeh wants us to be even more traditional than we already are," she said.

How the two of them could possibly get even more traditional than they already were was beyond me, but I didn't want to interrupt by asking.

"And when I married him and put on the wig . . . I guess I didn't realize that meant forever. I mean, I knew it meant forever, but not really. And now it's been nine years . . . and . . . and . . . and now regular kosher isn't even good enough for him anymore. He wants us to be *glatt* kosher."

I didn't understand the ramifications of being *glatt* kosher, but I figured it meant something like being kosher squared instead of just plain kosher. More rules to follow, that sort of thing. It meant Aryeh wanted more tradition while Alicia wanted less. How in the world were they going to solve this one?

"Does Aryeh know you took off the wig?"

She shook her head.

"Wow," I said.

"Yeah."

"Will he be mad?"

"I don't know," she said. "Yeah. He'll probably have a heart attack."

That sounded pretty close to right. Although a stroke was another possibility.

"Look. Maybe not. Maybe he'll be okay with it," I said, trying to sound convincing.

Alicia shook her head.

"No way," she said. "And, you know, Aryeh's not all that easy to get along with even when it's *not* Jewish stuff."

I nodded, even though this was all news to me.

"You've never told me that before," I said.

Alicia shrugged. "You've had a lot going on," she said. "Brian and everything."

She looked around my apartment for a little while, letting her eyes settle on different objects and furniture before moving on again.

"Pretty weird, huh?" she said finally.

"So, are you, like, not Orthodox anymore?"

"I'm still Orthodox. I just took off the wig. That's all. It's not the end of the world or anything."

"No. Of course not. End of the world? Geez, no."

"But don't tell anyone," she said.

"I won't."

She reached up and tugged on a short curl. "I have nice hair, don't I?"

"You do. You have very nice hair."

I put my arm around my sister, and she started to weep into my shoulder.

"God. Dammit," she said.

I ran my hand over my sister's head. Her real hair was silky fine, like a small child's.

"It's okay," I said.

"This is the first time in nine years that I've gone out in public like this."

I pressed my forehead against hers and nodded.

"I feel like a five-year-old," she said. "Like I'm going to get in trouble."

"I really don't think God cares all that much about the wig part," I said. "Not that I'd know or anything."

"Not in trouble with *God*. With *Aryeh*."

"Oh. Well, you can still wear it at home, right? When you and Aryeh do . . . Jewish stuff?"

Alicia lifted her head.

"Can we not talk about it?" she said. "Can we, like, watch a movie or something?"

Absolutely," I said.

I reached for my pile of DVDs and knocked through them until I found what I was looking for.

"A little Lloyd Dobler?" I asked.

Alicia smiled. We'd always shared a major celluloid crush on the keymaster.

"Absolutely," my sister said.

# 12

Just after the dinner rush at Sammy's Place, my mother showed up out of the blue. I spotted her standing next to the hostess's station in the purple trench coat, scanning the room with wide eyes.

"I'll be right with you," I said to an impatient table of four who'd been waiting a good twenty minutes for me to take their order. They could wait longer. Nothing worse than dinner patrons in a hurry, the husbands twisting their heads this way and that in a desperate attempt to catch your attention. More than once I'd felt like telling some jerk about the McDonald's two blocks down the road, where dinner would miraculously be waiting for them even before they'd ordered. But when you lived for tips, you learned to keep your big mouth shut. Most of the time.

"Mom," I said.

"Oh, there you are," my mother said.

"What's going on? Did something happen?"

"Nothing happened."

"What are you doing here?" I asked.

Maybe she'd broken things off with Ron and rushed over to give me the news.

"What am I doing here? I'm eating here. Ronald's parking the car. You go on. We'll ask for your section."

"You're *eating* here?"

"You want us to leave?"

"No. No. You just don't come here. Ever. But great. Stay."

I headed back to the impatient table of four, took their order, ran it to the kitchen, and came out to find my mother seated in a prime booth, Ron by her side, closely studying the menu through his thick glasses. Across from them, to my amazement and horror, sat the bareheaded Chaim/Chuck, who was currently thanking the busboy for filling their water glasses. Was I dumbfounded by this plan of attack on my mother's part? Not really. If anything, I felt a twinge of disappointment that I hadn't foreseen the entire scenario. Of course my mother would show up unannounced at Sammy's Place with the entirely available and clearly not balding Chaim/Chuck, sit in my section, and pretend everything was perfectly copacetic. This was my mother, after all.

"Hey, Ron," I said. "Hey, *Chaim*."

Chuck smiled at me and gave a tiny, embarrassed shrug, as if to say none of this had been his idea, please don't stab him with a steak knife.

"Well, Chaim hadn't eaten yet and so we invited him to join us, didn't we, Ronald?" my mother said.

Ron looked up from the menu. "Excuse me?" he said.

My mother patted Ron's arm.

"She called you?" I asked Chuck.

"Yeah," he said.

"Oh, God," I said.

Clearly, my mother had asked Alicia for Chuck's phone number—a fact Alicia had conveniently avoided passing along to me. By now, the entire Orthodox community was probably abuzz with my future wedding plans. Thankfully, besides my sister and her nuclear clan, I didn't know anyone else in the Orthodox community.

"Go ahead and do your thing," my mother said. "We don't want to keep you."

"This *is* my thing. You're in my section. And please don't make me tell you the specials."

"Oh, right. Well, give us a minute, then. Unless you know what you want, Chaim?"

"Uh, no. Not really."

"Well, you just take your time, isn't that right, Ronald? No rush."

Chuck blanched visibly behind his menu.

Ron tilted his face up toward mine.

"What're the specials tonight?" he asked.

I looked at my mother.

"I'll be right back," I said.

---

I ignored the three stooges in the prime booth for as long as I possibly could before finally returning with their dinner salads, my mother's with dressing on the side.

"So, Chaim was just telling us about his family," my mother said.

She immediately eyed the lettuce, never trusting for a moment that the prep crew had properly washed the produce.

"Great," I said.

I raised my eyebrows at Chuck and he smiled back at me, a little sheepish smile that meant the error in judgment he'd made in accepting my mother's invitation to dinner had become crystal clear. Well, it was too late. They still had steak and potatoes to get through. And probably dessert. That's what he got for picking up the phone when it rang.

"He's one of five children!" my mother said.

She shook her head in disbelief, as though being one of five children were somehow an unusual and fascinating feat, on a par with being a trapeze artist or winning the Nobel Peace Prize. As though her very own daughter didn't have five children herself.

I felt a little sorry for Chuck right then. But I must say, he demonstrated amazing perseverance. Each time I glanced at their table, he was deep into conversation with both Ron and my mother and acting as though he'd rather be nowhere else. In his slightly tattered, blue button-down shirt that had clearly never seen an iron, he looked just like the starving, aspiring young filmmaker that he was. And I must say, it was a pretty good look. I wondered if he'd worked hard at picking his outfit for the evening or if he'd merely pulled things out of his drawers at random. Did he know he looked disheveled? Or was his disheveled appearance the real thing? I liked a guy who appeared as though he never looked in a mirror, but when a guy looked into a mirror in order to achieve the no-look-in-the-mirror look, it ruined everything. Not that I'd set my sights on Chuck. But it seemed possible that he'd set his sights on me, a fact that gave my bruised ego a much needed boost. I might not have been a long-haired, long-legged, mountain-climbing veterinarian, but I could still get a guy in a wrinkled shirt to pay attention to me. Unless, of course, he'd merely been hungry and known better than to turn down a free meal.

"Listen," my mother said when I delivered the bill to Ron. "Ronald and I have got to get moving—a movie. Downtown. Do you think you could give Chaim here a ride home? After your shift?"

"Oh, no, you don't have to do that," Chuck said. "Really. I don't need a ride."

"But of course you do!"

"I can . . . walk. Or catch a bus or something."

"No, no. Rena will drive you. She doesn't mind."

"That's all right," Chuck said.

"Don't you get off soon?" my mother asked me.

She had desperation written all over her face. She looked

like a little girl about to open the very last birthday present, hoping with all her might it will somehow miraculously turn out to be the very thing she wanted.

"I've got another forty-five minutes," I said. "Give or take."

"That's not so long," my mother said.

"Or we can drop him off," Ron said.

My mother slapped him audibly on the thigh.

"No, no. Rena's got it taken care of," she said. "Haven't you, Rena?"

I plucked the remaining plates and glasses from their table and held them aloft. What the hell. I'd make my mother deliriously happy.

"Would you like a ride home in forty-five minutes, Chaim?" I asked.

Chuck looked from my face to my mother's and back to mine again.

"You know what? I'll catch a cab home. It's fine."

"No, no. I'll take you," I said.

"I'll catch a cab. Really. I should be going soon anyway."

"We'll take him," Ron said.

"I'd be happy to drive you home," I said. "Really. Not a problem."

Chuck shrugged and looked at me.

"Okay," he said.

I'm nearly positive my mother mentally crossed herself and thanked Jesus.

"Perfect!" she said.

---

I drive the dirtiest Subaru in the western hemisphere. Do not argue with me on that one. Do not claim to have an even dirtier, smellier, more disgusting Subaru than mine. You cannot win. Yes, sure, you have kids, a dog, a few stained remnants of spilled sodas, a sandwich or two lost under the seats. I scoff at your meager messes. My Subaru is worse. My Subaru beats your Subaru hands down. Do I take pride in the sordid state of my car? Not really. I'm just not motivated enough to clean it up.

Besides, over the years, I've found that a dirty car provides the perfect litmus test for forming new friendships. For instance, if a new acquaintance has to be warned several times on the walk to the Subaru about what sight/smell/stickiness awaits them, then I already know that the new acquaintance is out of my league and will never be invited into my apartment for a glass of flat Diet Coke. If I feel compelled to give the warning only twice, the person has a much better chance. If I give only one warning, and especially if that person sits in my car and exclaims, "This is nothing! My car is worse!" (an impossibility, but still an outburst that is always welcomed), then a budding friendship may be in the cards. But if no warning comes—if I feel no compunction whatsoever about the raging tornado of debris that awaits the person I've offered a ride to—well, that, my friend, is a surefire sign that a friendship is in the making. Either that or I just don't give a shit about the person at all.

All of which is to say it was probably a good sign that it didn't occur to me to warn Chuck about my car. I didn't even think about it until he was already safely settled in the front seat next to me, having shoved several magazines, papers, bags, pens, and empty water bottles onto the floor.

"Sorry, my car's kind of a mess," I said then.

Chuck shrugged. "I've seen worse," he said.

"I've noticed you're a big shrugger," I said.

"A what?"

"A shrugger. You shrug your shoulders a lot."

I shrugged my shoulders to demonstrate. He shrugged me back.

"It's a good all-purpose answer," he said.

I shrugged.

"Look," he said. "You should know that your mother sort of said you'd asked me to come to the restaurant. I thought we were all meeting for dinner."

"Oh, God."

"So, I'm sorry for, you know, showing up like that. It's pretty embarrassing, really."

"I'm the one who's embarrassed. God, my mother! I'm so sorry!"

"No, I'm sorry."

"I'm going to kill her."

"I think she meant well."

"Yeah, well, she's not your mother."

"True."

"Okay, deep breaths," I said.

I inhaled once and blew out the air. Would a day ever come when my mother would leave me alone? I knew the answer to that question already.

"It's okay," he said. "I mean, I could have said no."

"True."

"So. Sorry."

"Not your fault," I said.

"Okay, so everything's okay."

"Yeah."

"Good."

"Right."

I started up the car.

"So, where do you live, anyway?" I asked him.

"Green Lake."

I backed out of the parking space.

"But would you like to get a drink somewhere first? Or coffee?" Chuck asked.

I shrugged. I was more than a little flattered. But truth was, I really had to get home and take the Big Guy out. I'd learned from short experience, the Big Guy didn't take kindly to hours cooped up in my apartment.

"I'd like to, but I can't," I said.

"Oh."

"I've got a dog in my apartment and he's got to go out."

"What kind of dog do you have?"

"A yellow lab. And he's not mine. I'm actually just taking care of him for a little while. Dog-sitting."

"That's nice of you."

I shrugged. "Not really," I said.

"Well, we could take the dog out first and then you wouldn't have to worry about taking him out."

I tried to remember just what state I'd left my apartment in. The problem is that when your place is in a shambles for long enough, it starts to look normal to you. Still, I couldn't remember the last time I'd vacuumed the floors or washed the dishes that had piled up in the kitchen sink, or done just about anything else that could be construed as cleaning, for that matter. I'm pretty certain your average person would place the state of my apartment somewhere on the cleanliness scale between shocking and appalling.

"My apartment's not too clean," I told him.

He shrugged. "How dirty can it be?"

"Very."

"I'm sure it's not that bad. I mean, just look at how neat you keep your car."

I smiled. "Okay. Don't say I didn't warn you."

"I'll consider myself warned," he said.

I pulled out into the street. What do you say to the person you hardly know who is riding in the seat next to you in your car? The fine art of appropriate small talk has always been beyond me. And silence makes me nervous.

"So, Chuck," I said. "What's the worst thing you've ever done?"

It was the best I could come up with on the spot, probably since I was well aware that the worst thing I'd ever done was about to introduce his slobbery self to my unsuspecting passenger.

"What do you mean?"

"Well, like, have you ever robbed a bank? Or stolen a gumball? Or tripped a blind person?"

"I've tripped *two* blind people."

"No, really."

"What? Is this some kind of personality test?"

"Yes. Like if you were to tell me you've killed somebody, then I might consider making you get out at the next light."

"Oh, very good way to suss out the murderers."

"So, what is it?"

"Okay. Let's see. Worst thing. Hmmm."

"Slept with a married woman?"

"That counts?"

"Come on. You're acting like this is a game or something."

"Oh, right. Let me get serious."

He put a hand up to his bearded chin and stroked it. "Well, I'm not very consistent in my flossing," he said.

"You are very bad at this."

"Okay, then you tell me. What's the worst thing you've ever done?"

I thought about telling him then and there about the Big Guy but quickly came to my senses. Even though I knew he was only Chuck and not the religious Chaim I'd first thought him to be, I still didn't want to smudge my appearance in front of the only man currently paying me any attention. What if he thought stealing the Big Guy made me a terrible person? Because, in fact, stealing the Big Guy *did* more or less make me a terrible person. Except that I wasn't a terrible person underneath it all. Just a seriously messed-up one.

"I'm a perfect angel," I said.

"That's what I thought," Chuck said.

# 13

By the time we arrived at my apartment building, walked up the three flights of stairs, and stood at the threshold of the door I was about to open, I'd come to my senses. No person, no matter how nonjudgmental, could possibly witness the state of my apartment and not come to the conclusion that I had serious issues.

"Maybe you'd better wait out here," I said.

Chuck pushed on the door and peered inside.

"Okay, you weren't kidding," he said.

"You definitely wait out here," I said. "I'll get the dog."

"Oh, no, no. I'll . . . manage."

He tiptoed through the pile of clothes greeting him at the front door.

"Interesting closet system," he said. "What do you use the closet for?"

"No smart-ass comments."

I switched on a couple of lights, and the stark, full-on,

complete, and utterly senseless mess of my daily world revealed itself in living color. I tried to fathom the impression my apartment might be making on Chuck. Was there any chance on earth that any normal person would find my total lack of discipline charming? No, there wasn't.

"There he is," I said, pointing at the Big Guy, hoping he'd provide a bit of much needed distraction.

The worst watchdog of all time lay sound asleep, sprawled out across the center of my sheetless bed, his lump of a head resting on my pillow.

"Is he alive?" Chuck asked.

The Big Guy opened his eyes, looked at the both of us, and then closed them again.

"Here we go, boy," I said. "Come on. Let's go."

"What's his name?"

"Big Guy. Come on, Big Guy, here we go, now."

The Big Guy ignored me.

"Well trained," Chuck said.

"Come on, you."

I grabbed the dog by his purple collar and pulled. No movement.

"Guess he's not too desperate to go out," I said.

After that, I didn't know what to do. I made a sweep of the room with my eyes, in search of dirty underwear or bras with sweat stains. None to be seen—my only stroke of luck so far.

"You want something to drink?" I asked. The second the words came out of my mouth, I regretted them. With any luck, Chuck would telepathically understand my error and say no.

"Sure," he said.

He followed me into the kitchen. At one time—say, when I first moved in—the kitchen was actually quite cute, with its built-in breakfast nook, sunny yellow walls, and the brand-new white porcelain sink my dad had given me as a move-in present. But I'd slowly and with great success completely concealed the cuteness factor. It didn't help that more than once, without an inch of clear counter space on which to set a pot, I'd simply opened a drawer, deposited said pot, and then left it there, more or less permanently.

"Wow," Chuck said.

I sighed. "I've been a bit low lately. Distracted. Not too motivated to clean up, I guess."

"I guess not."

I opened the fridge.

"Okay, you've got your choice of . . . water. Or Diet Coke, no bubbles. Or water."

"I'll take water."

"Excellent choice. Let's go to a restaurant and order some."

"What about the dog?"

"Well, I suppose we should rouse him and take him out."

Chuck clapped his hands, and miraculously the Big Guy came to life. I hadn't tried the clapping hands trick before. Chuck clipped on the leash and the dog walked merrily to the door. We stepped out into the hall.

"Look," I said. "Before we go down the stairs I have to

warn you. We were very, very lucky to have avoided seeing the super on the way up. But there's no way we're going to be that lucky twice. So when he comes out to talk to us, just follow my lead and keep walking. It's going to seem really, really rude, but trust me on this one."

"Got it. Trust you."

"Rena?" Derrick called just then from down a flight of stairs. "Is that you?"

I looked at Chuck. I looked at the dog. Did Derrick know Brian's dog? Would he recognize the Big Guy? Was the jig up? I looked at Chuck again.

"Yeah!" I called back.

"Hey, what's going on, girl?"

"Oh! Not much!"

Chuck started down the stairs, still holding on to the Big Guy's leash.

"Just a second," I said in a stage whisper to Chuck.

I set a hand on his shoulder.

"You want to get a beer with me?" Derrick called.

"No thanks! Got company! But thanks anyway!"

"Another time, then!"

"Okay. See ya!"

"Who's that?" Chuck whispered.

"Neighbor," I whispered back.

I listened for Derrick's door to close but didn't hear anything.

"Um, I forgot something," I whispered to Chuck. "Be right back, okay?"

"Sure."

I turned around, headed back to my apartment, stepped inside, counted slowly to ten, and then returned to Chuck on the stairs. I figured by then Derrick would be gone and I could avoid finding out if he recognized the Big Guy. I figured wrong.

"Hey!" Derrick said.

He was standing on the second-floor landing. Damn it. I should have known he'd want to see who my company was. Derrick looked from Chuck to the dog to me to Chuck to the dog again. He didn't say anything. If it was curtains on the entire escapade, he certainly was taking his own sweet time letting me know. Finally, he looked up at Chuck.

"Nice dog, man," he said.

Chuck smiled at him.

Derrick raised his eyebrows at me.

"Now, don't you kids stay out too late," he said.

"Thanks, Dad," I said.

I would have sighed with relief at the bullet I'd just dodged were it not for the fact that we still had Carl to deal with. Like clockwork, Carl came lunging out just as Chuck and I passed through the alcove. He had a shiny brown smudge on his white shirt that I recognized immediately as the brown gravy that accompanies the brown turkey in the single-serving Swanson TV dinners Carl lived off of. He still held his fork in his hand, an implement he brandished in front of him like a miniature billy club.

"Say!" he shouted. "What have we here?"

"Hello," Chuck said.

I kept moving briskly toward the exit, the Big Guy by my side.

"See you later, Carl!" I shouted.

"That dog still here?" Carl thundered.

"He's on his way out! Really! I promise!"

"Heard that one before! And who's this con artist?"

He pointed at Chuck with the fork.

"Who, me?" Chuck asked.

"You see anybody else here?"

"I'm a friend of Rena's. Chuck."

He thrust his hand out toward Carl, and Carl shook it.

"Nice to meet you," Chuck said.

"How do you know?" Carl said. He let out a loud snicker at his own joke.

"Good point," Chuck said.

"Say," Carl said. "You look like a smart enough fellow. Tell me, how many watts of electricity does it take to operate one single hair dryer?"

"Can't say as I know."

This was a perfect example of why the building's tenants learned very quickly to keep moving past Carl. The man simply plucked topics from the air and then ran with them. In my first few months, I'd tried my best to stay until the bitter end, just to be polite. But Carl had absolutely no sense of the norms of conversation. Somewhere along the line, he'd missed the part where the other person takes a turn to say something.

"Here's what happens," Carl was saying. "Folks don't think

about stuff like this. They plug their hair dryers into the wall and just let 'em go. And now it's the guys, too. Not just the ladies. Who needs a hair dryer, anyway? For centuries, we all got by just fine letting our hairs dry in the breeze."

"Gotta go, Chuck," I said. "We're late."

"Did you know that the forces of evolution are slowly turning humans into hairless beings?" Carl asked.

I grabbed Chuck by the elbow and shoved him out toward the door.

"Sure, you got that fuzz on your chin now. But a century from today—"

"Guess we have to go," Chuck said. "Maybe you can tell me more later."

"Five more days!" Carl yelled after me.

"What does he mean? Five more days?" Chuck asked when we were on the sidewalk.

"Oh, the Big Guy. No dogs allowed in the building."

"How much longer are you taking care of him?"

"Don't ask," I said.

Upping his friendship quotient by at least one hundred points, Chuck didn't flinch when I suggested the International House of Pancakes for coffee. Brian wouldn't go near an IHOP to save his life. The few times early on in our relationship when I'd managed to bribe him into late-night pancakes, he'd fretted the whole time about what he perceived to be the scary yet invisible goings-on behind the restaurant kitchen door.

"So, why didn't you become an actress?" Chuck asked, sitting across from me in a turquoise booth, a plastic pot of coffee on the table between us. We'd left the Big Guy behind to sleep in the car.

"Did I say I wanted to be an actress?"

"Aviva did. At dinner Friday night."

"Oh, right. Well, I'm sure I would have been a great actress, but unfortunately, I'm lacking all talent."

"How do you know?"

"Oh, I know. I can't act my way out of a paper bag."

"Have you tried?"

"Acting my way out of a paper bag?"

"You know what I mean."

"I tried a few plays in high school and, basically, I sucked."

"You can't say you sucked based on a few high school plays."

"I beg to differ. You didn't see me."

"Well, everybody sucks in high school."

I looked inside of my empty coffee cup. The white ceramic bottom was covered in scratches. Probably a thousand spoons had stirred coffee inside of that cup.

"I actually meant to be a drama major in college," I said. "I took a couple of classes. But, I don't know. I didn't keep going."

Chuck picked up the coffeepot and filled our cups. How I wished I had something else to tell him—that I worked in regional theater and was currently in between projects or that

I was moving to New York City in another week for an audition.

"What happened?" Chuck asked.

"I don't know. The other people in my classes, they were so . . . theatrical. Like they lived and breathed the whole thing. Born on the stage, or something. They were those kids in high school who did every play. The nerdy theater kids. And I just . . . well, I didn't really fit in."

"I bet you were as good as any of them."

I opened two sugar packets, dumped the sugar into my coffee, and then stirred it with a spoon, making sure to scrape the bottom of the cup.

"And you make movies," I said, just to change the subject.

"Well, yeah. I don't usually admit to that. I mean, everybody and his brother's a filmmaker now. But, yeah, I want to make movies. Right now, I'm studying them, you know? Watching all kinds of films and dissecting them to see how it's done."

If I'd had any inclination to tell Chuck about the Kurt Russell Weekend I'd had the month before, he'd just now quashed it.

"It seems like that would sort of ruin the experience," I said.

"Really it's just the opposite. It makes watching a movie fascinating. If you pay close enough attention, you can see the director thinking. You can see all of the tiny decisions that went into every scene."

I could hear it in his voice, the excitement he felt for cinema. The serious approach he took to his art. It was funny, but in that moment he sort of reminded me of Brian and the way Brian used to talk about his climbing trips—with complete enthusiasm. God, I was envious. In comparison, my own life seemed awfully boring and inconsequential.

"Okay, so what's your favorite movie?" I asked.

"My personal favorite?"

I nodded.

"I'd have to say *Chinatown*. Or else *The Godfather.* But it changes. Sometimes, I think *The Graduate*. Not too original, I suppose. But I can't help it. A great movie is a great movie. Of course, the greatest movie ever made is *Citizen Kane*."

"Never seen it."

"You've never seen *Citizen Kane*? How can that be? How can you have gone your whole life and not seen *Citizen Kane*? That's just insane."

"I don't know. I guess I was just . . . watching something else."

"We're going to have to fix that. God, I can't let you go another week without watching that movie. I'm bringing it over and we're watching it."

"Okay, okay."

Chuck poured cream into his coffee, took a sip, and then added more cream.

"So. New topic," he said. "Why are you so depressed?"

"Did I say I was depressed?"

"More or less."

"Oh. Well, I guess I am."

"Like chronically?"

"Not really."

Someone had etched the words *Suzy+Hal 4-EVER* into the Formica tabletop. Was there any chance on earth that dear Suzy and Hal were still together? I doubted it.

"So, what is it? Free-flowing depression? Or something more specific?"

"Something more specific."

"You don't have to tell me."

"Okay."

"Unless you want to."

"Okay."

I didn't say anything.

"So, what is it?"

I smiled.

"Well. My boyfriend—excuse me, former boyfriend—excuse me, former fiancé—changed his mind and decided he didn't want to marry me."

"I'm sorry."

"Yeah, well, it wouldn't be so bad, except that he moved in with another woman before he even told me we'd broken up. God. I had to hear it from his *dad*, of all people."

"How long did you go out?"

"Oh, a while. Not long."

"A year?"

"Seven. Seven years. Pretty much."

"Seven years?"

"Yeah."

"That's a long time."

"I suppose so. But I'm over him now. O-ver."

Four huge and clearly stoned teenage boys jostled their way into the next booth, slapping at one another and arguing over who was going to sit next to whom. After a moment, they all shut up and stared at the menus.

"The longest I ever went out with someone was two years," Chuck said. "Glenda Waters."

"And what became of Glenda Waters?"

"Married Stephen Orrey."

I nodded.

"Chocolate-chip pancakes. Man, that's what I'm getting," one of the teenage boys said.

"And are they still married?" I asked.

"Brand-new-baby married. House in the suburbs. The whole nine yards."

"Stephen Fucking Orrey."

"No, he's all right."

Chuck picked up a packet of sugar, tore it open, and poured the sugar into a tiny pile onto the table.

"You thinking of licking that up?" I asked.

He opened another packet, poured the new sugar on top of the first pile of sugar, then started to make circles in the sugar with his finger. It made me think of a bunch of Tibetan monks I'd seen one night when I somehow ended up zoned out in front of the Discovery Channel. What the monks did was make this incredibly elaborate design out of different colors of sand. They worked very slowly and meticulously for days, and they couldn't breathe while they worked, because they might blow the sand by mistake and wreck the design. Which is sort of ironic since the whole point of making the design in the first place was to wreck it when it was finished. Which is what they did. The monks had this ceremony where they played Tibetan instruments and then they blew all of the sand into one tiny pile. Of course, the whole thing was a metaphor for our own temporary existences, but you know what? I really didn't need the reminder of how we'll all be returning to dust one day. I guess that's what I get for watching the Discovery Channel.

I watched Chuck play with the sugar for a minute. It looked sort of fun. I grabbed a few packets of sugar myself and dumped the contents onto the table in front of me.

"You know what really gets me?" I asked, drawing my own circles.

"What's that?"

"Me and Brian never even lived together. And in two seconds he's living with someone else."

Chuck nodded.

"And a dog."

Chuck nodded some more.

"The Big Guy, in fact. The Big Guy's their dog."

"And now you're doggy-sitting him? God, that's nice of you."

"Well, they don't exactly know I'm doggy-sitting him."

Chuck looked at me. "They don't?" he asked.

I shook my head. "No," I said. "They don't."

"Excuse me if this is a stupid question. But, then, what are you doing with him?"

I thought about what to say. I had terrible timing: Out of the blue, Chuck was suddenly looking like potential boyfriend material, or at least potential sleeping-with material, and there I was, blowing everything. Still, honesty seemed the best policy.

"I stole him?"

"You stole him?"

"Yes."

One of the teenage boys in the next booth turned his head to glance at me. I waved at him. Chuck nodded. Then he knocked on the table a couple of times. He folded his arms across his chest, leaned back, and looked at me.

"Aryeh said you were unique," he said.

"He did?" I couldn't believe that my sister's husband would say anything complimentary about me. "And he meant that in a good way, right?"

"I don't think he knows about your criminal tendencies."

I nodded.

"Well, at least I didn't murder my old boyfriend," I said. "Although, I did consider it."

Chuck swept all of his sugar into one pile, cupped one palm at the edge of the countertop, and then swept the whole pile into his cupped hand. He looked at me.

"Okay, so you're still a little bit mad at him," he said.

"That's one way to put it."

Here are the things I learned about Chuck that night: He grew up in New York City. He met Aryeh at the gym, playing basketball. He loves movies. He came west in order to get out of the East. He likes the great outdoors in concept but isn't much of an outdoorsy guy. He supports himself filming weddings and bar mitzvahs while he studies the art of filmmaking. And he'd agreed to dinner with my mother and Ron because he'd wanted to see me again.

Here are the things Chuck learned about me: I'm a slob. I'm a waitress in a steakhouse with no future career prospects. I have a very pushy mother. I have one major failed relationship under my belt. I have no confidence in myself. I'm a criminal.

You do the math.

# 14

The next morning, I was suddenly very popular. First, Derrick called and asked if maybe I'd like to have dinner, and I asked him if he meant, like, a dinner date, and he kind of hemmed and hawed and then said, yeah, he guessed so, and so I told him I didn't want to go out on a date with him, to which he said, not a date, then, to which I said, too late.

Then my old high school friend Gloria called to tell me I had no choice, the old high school posse was going out for drinks the next night and I was coming along, no excuses, to which I said, all right, I'll come.

Then Lisa called to see if maybe I wanted to meet her someplace for breakfast, and I said I couldn't because I still needed an hour or two more of sleep, but I'd probably be up for lunch if she wanted to try me again later.

Then, just as I was nodding off on the sofa, someone knocked on my door. It couldn't be a friend—only someone who didn't know me well enough to simply walk into my apartment would bother to knock. With my luck, I'd move from my comfortably warm spot next to the Big Guy only to find a couple of Jehovah's Witnesses at my door, holding Bibles. No, thank you.

"Rena!" I heard my mother call.

This was a surprise. Not the fact that it was my mother who'd come to visit—members of my family have a tendency to show up at my apartment whenever they're in the neighborhood, a seemingly constant occurrence. No, it was that my mother rarely, if ever, actually ventured up the stairs to my apartment. She preferred the stop-in-front-of-my-building-and-honk method—a method that, I must admit, was pretty effective. Especially since my mother felt no apprehension about leaning on the horn and yelling out her car window until I finally responded. Needless to say, Carl wasn't my mother's biggest fan, along with a few dozen of my neighbors.

"Just a second," I said.

I walked to the door and opened it a crack, just enough to see my mother hovering anxiously on the other side, wearing what at first looked to be a pair of pajamas but on closer inspection turned out to be a baby blue velour tracksuit. I made a mental note to remind myself that if I ever became involved with another man in this lifetime, I wouldn't start wearing velour tracksuits.

"Hello, Mother," I said through the slight opening of the door.

"You want me to stand in the hallway?" she said.

"I'm not speaking to you."

"Rena, come on. Let me in. Open the door."

"Not after you dumped Chuck—*Chaim*—on me last night."

"Dumped him? Rena! Honey! You offered him a ride home!"

"I didn't offer him a ride home. You told me to drive him home."

"Let your mother in. You're going to yell at me, at least let me come in first."

I pulled the door open wide and gave her a good look at the state of my living room.

"Oh," she said.

She hesitated a moment before regaining her composure.

"Okay," she said. "Well, I came to take you out for coffee. Or whatever. I have something I want to talk with you about. Wait a second, did you get a dog?"

We both looked over at the Big Guy, who had decided to rouse himself and head over to the door to see what all the commotion was about. He stared first at my mother and then at me, then back to my mother again, as though searching for any familial resemblance. I patted him on the back and he sat.

"Oh. Yeah," I said.

"You got a dog and you didn't tell me?"

"I just got him."

"Oh. Well. Where should we go? How about Starbucks? We can go someplace else if you'd rather. Do you know a place? Maybe we should just go to Starbucks. Do you think?"

"Just come in, Mom. I don't feel like putting on shoes and going out."

"Well, all right. I won't stay long. Really I won't. I've got a million things to do."

My mother took a step inside the door.

"God, Rena. The way you live!"

She squinted as though looking at my apartment were as painful to her vision as looking directly into the sun.

"Maybe you'd better just tell me whatever it is you want to tell me," I said.

"Okay," she said.

"Okay."

"I want you to come to dinner on Sunday. If you can. You don't work this coming Sunday, do you?"

I did. But it would be easy enough to get Sunday night off.

"That's it? That's why you bothered to park the car and walk up three flights of stairs?" I asked.

"I want you to be there when I tell your father that Ronald and I have gotten engaged."

"You what?" I asked.

"We're getting married," she said.

She beamed at me her beaming smile, the one where she looks like a six-year-old waiting for the applause she knows is coming following her interminable tap dance at the first-grade talent show.

"You're kidding," I said.

"Not kidding."

Prepared as I should have been to hear this piece of news,

I was thrown completely off guard. Up until that moment, I'd still thought it possible we were all playing one big game together—a game Ron was set to lose from the start. I looked at my mother's hand for concrete evidence.

"You're not wearing a ring," I said.

"Well, aren't you the detective! We're having rings made. Matching rings with our initials on them. Silver. You'll see. Pretty. We didn't want to go that old diamond route, you know. We want something different."

"Right," I said.

I didn't know what to say. When my mother was married to my father, she wore a diamond that once belonged to his grandmother. I wondered where that old diamond route of a ring was now.

"So," I said. "When's the . . . ceremony?"

"In the spring," she said. "After Ronald finishes his conversion class."

I nodded.

"Isn't that great?" my mother said.

"Well, God. Gosh. Yes. Great. Congratulations."

"Thank you, honey."

"Wow," I said. "You're really going to marry Ron. That's really something."

"Why is that really something?"

"It just . . . is. Getting married. To Ron. It's really something."

"It *is* something, isn't it?"

We both nodded.

"So, Dad doesn't know?"

My mother scrunched up her face and shook her head.

"Poor Dad. He was hoping the whole Ron thing would pass," I said.

My mother sighed. "I wish you wouldn't call it that. 'The whole Ron thing.'"

"I didn't mean it in a bad way."

My mother pursed her lips again, tightly. "Look. I'm hoping with you there, and Alicia, maybe he'll handle the news better, you know?"

"Maybe you should just call and tell him. Avoid a big dramatic scene."

"I don't want him to hear it over the phone. I don't think that's right. I don't. I think he needs to hear it in person."

"But couldn't you at least tell him without Ron there?"

"I wouldn't feel right about that, either. Ronald needs to be there. Your father is just going to have to get used to it."

I thought it was a terrible idea all the way around, but I nodded anyway.

"Yeah, okay," I said.

"So, you'll do it?"

"I don't want to. But I will."

"Great," my mother said.

"Do not invite Chaim."

"I wasn't going to invite Chaim."

"I mean it, Mother. No Chaim."

I didn't need any more meddling in my nonexistent love life from my mother.

"Got it. No Chaim."

"And no other single guys."

"Right."

"No discussion of single guys."

"No discussion."

"No mention of my single status in any way, shape, or form."

"Rena, I think I get the point."

"All right, I'll be there."

"Oh, great. You're a good girl. But your place . . . God, Rena. How can you live like this?"

After my mother left, I sat on the couch with the Big Guy again and tried to be happy for my mother. Why shouldn't I be happy? She'd found herself a new husband to love and grow old with. How great was that? Just because the new husband had turned out to be Ron shouldn't be an issue. The only issue was my mother's happiness. Still, her score of two marriages to my zero kind of sucked.

"I can't believe my mother's marrying that serial killer," I said to the Big Guy.

I called Alicia, who answered on the first ring.

"So you heard about Mom," she said.

"I heard."

"Poor Dad."

"I know."

"She loves him, I guess," Alicia said.

"I guess so."

Silence.

"He's all right," Alicia said.

I made a grunting noise.

Silence.

"Well," she said finally.

"So," I said. I couldn't wait any longer for Alicia to bring up the subject of her wig. "How's, you know, everything?"

"I don't know," she said. "All right. Sort of. Not really."

"You want to come over?"

"Can't."

"Okay," I said.

Silence.

"You want me to come over there?"

"Not right now. Really. It's okay."

"Okay. So. Sunday."

"Yeah," she said.

"You'd better be there."

"*You'd* better be there."

Silence again.

"Okay," I said.

"All right."

"Sunday, then."

"Yeah, Sunday."

And we hung up at the same time.

# 15

It occurred to me that returning the dog might very well solve everything. After all, if Brian was so damn happy to have the dog go missing, then maybe having the dog magically reappear would throw a wrench into his charmed life. Maybe that wrench would even be heavy enough to conk the living daylights out of his charmed relationship with Anna. Maybe I could ruin everything. Besides, I didn't want to get kicked out of my apartment for breaking the dog rules. But—nondecider that I am—I decided to table the decision until later. And then, because basically I'm a nice enough person, I called up my dad and asked if he'd like to go for a walk. Maybe I'd break my mother's news to him, save him the punch in the gut he was surely going to feel Sunday night.

I grabbed the Big Guy and his leash, ran through the alcove before Carl could catch my eye, piled the dog into my car, and twenty minutes later found my dad standing in the parking lot at Green Lake, looking very happy to see me.

"You got a dog!" he shouted.

"Yeah," I said.

The Big Guy was busy sniffing at the leash with his wet nose.

"He won't bite?"

My dad fears the wrath of dogs the way little kids fear the dark. Even the most calm dog—asleep in front of the fire, too old to rouse himself at the sight of a stranger—puts my dad in a panic. The story goes that he'd once been bitten as a child and had never recovered from the trauma.

"He's world's sweetest dog," I said. "Go ahead. Pet him."

"What's his name?"

"Big Guy."

In an unusual show of strength, Al reached a tentative black-gloved hand toward the Big Guy's head and patted him lightly once.

"Hello there, Big Guy," he said. He stood up straight again. "Say, let me get a picture."

"Oh, Dad. No."

"Come on. One picture. I got a new camera. A digital."

I didn't need any photographic evidence of stolen property in my possession, but it wasn't as if Brian were planning on spending an afternoon any time in the near future perusing my dad's photo albums.

"Oh, all right," I said.

I stood with the Big Guy by my side and smiled for my dad's new digital camera.

"Got it," he said. "All set."

He tucked the camera into a coat pocket, and we walked together along the asphalt path that encircles the lake. The place was unusually empty of joggers and roller skaters for an afternoon in October. Overhead, the usual mattress of dark clouds sagged, threatening to drop their rainy load at any moment.

We talked for a bit—my dad caught me up on our cousins in California and my great-aunt in the nursing home and various other relatives and friends he thought I should know about, and then, out of the blue and unconnected to anything else, he said, "You aren't yourself lately."

"Where did that come from?" I asked.

"I don't know. You just aren't."

I shrugged. "I guess I'm not," I said.

I stuffed my fists into the pockets of my down vest. To our left, the water was the color of metal.

"You know, I never really cared much for that Brian," he said.

I stopped walking, and a moment later, when he noticed I was no longer beside him, so did Al. He turned around and looked at me.

"I'm sorry," he said. "It's just the truth. Honey, he wasn't in your . . . class, you know?"

"My class? What do you mean by that?"

"Look, nice enough guy, that Brian. But you're so much smarter. You've got so much more going for you."

"I don't know about that."

What was it with the men in my life? Why was it that both

my dad and my ex-boyfriend seemed to think I had untapped potential lurking beneath my static surface? I lived in my body! There was no untapped potential lurking! Or if there was, it was doing an incredible job of hiding itself. We started walking again, more slowly now. The Big Guy sniffed at the edge of the path as we walked, his tail wagging.

"One thing I don't understand," Al said. "I don't understand why you stay at that restaurant year after year."

"You're really covering it all now," I said.

"I'm sorry. There's a lot on my mind when it comes to you. And it's true. I really don't understand why you keep that job."

"It pays."

"You know what I mean. Come on. You don't want to be a waitress for the rest of your life. If you're not going to come work with me . . . well, have you thought about seeing a career counselor? Take a few of those tests and find out what you're good at?"

"Maybe."

"If you ask me, you don't give yourself enough credit. You're very good at designing bathrooms. I know, I know, it's not the big glamorous job or anything, but didn't you enjoy putting together that bathroom in your apartment? And how about the powder room at your mother's? God, the compliments we've gotten on that one!"

When I was fifteen, my parents allowed me to choose everything for the redesign of the downstairs bathroom, and they'd both been talking as though it were the envy of the neighborhood ever since.

"Oh, Dad. You have not."

"It's true! It's very true. I'm not making it up."

"Whatever."

My dad shook his head. "And then you went into speech therapy. I never understood that one."

"It was a practical decision."

"Maybe. But you didn't stick with it. How practical is that?"

"I hated it, really."

"Life is way too short, honey. One day you wake up and it's all over."

"Dad."

"Well, it's true. We all die. And I don't want you to be dead and wondering why you didn't make more of your time here on earth."

"Do dead people wonder?"

"You know what I mean."

"Why are you so maudlin all of a sudden?"

"I'm just trying to be helpful. You seem . . . I don't know. Like you're waiting for something to happen. But you can't wait anymore, darling. And now with Brian gone—it's an opportunity, really. To do something with yourself."

"I thought you wanted me to wear nice clothes and go to nice places so I could meet a guy and marry him."

"Honey. I'm of a different generation. What can I say? It's

different now. I see that. And I just think you have so much ahead of you."

We walked for a while without saying anything. A group of older women in tracksuits powered past us, their middles uniformly thick above chopstick legs. Within seconds, they'd disappeared around a curve in the path. The Big Guy stopped to sniff at a tree and we gave him a moment before walking again. I was just wondering if now would be a good time to break my mother's news to my dad when he beat me to it.

"So, what do you think?" my dad said. "You think they'll go through with it?"

"Go through with what?"

"Getting married. Your mother thinks she's going to marry that doctor fellow."

"She told you that?"

"Not in so many words."

My father stopped. He slapped his forehead with the palm of one gloved hand.

"She's known him, what? Six months? It's crazy! How can she marry him?"

I didn't know what to say. I finally decided to give things as positive a spin as possible.

"Well, at least you and Mom still have the book group."

"Are you kidding? We quit that months ago. Ever since she met the doctor. Where have you been?"

I was wondering the same thing. So many things had

changed in my family in the last few months—it was almost like I'd been out of the country without a post office box or e-mail. Except that I hadn't been.

"She doesn't even know him," my dad continued. "He could turn out to be a nutcase. He could be one of those guys who stuffs women into suitcases and throws them into the ocean."

I avoided bringing up my own serial killer theory. It seemed unfair to Ron. He was a nice enough guy, after all. I was pretty sure he wasn't out to murder my mother.

"Dad, don't you think you're exaggerating a little bit?"

"No, I don't. I've got to look after her best interests, don't I? And this is not in her best interest."

It was touching to hear my dad talk about my mother in such a fashion. Also heartbreaking. He cared about her in a permanent way, through thick and thin, for richer, for poorer, till death do them part. That was the same way I felt about the traitorous Brian. I was pretty sure I'd love that guy forever.

"I think she's happy, Dad. I feel bad saying that to you, but I think maybe it's true."

My dad rocked back and forth on his feet. He wore the hiking boots my mother had purchased for him probably fifteen years before. They still looked new.

"That's a tough one," he said.

When I got back to my apartment, there was a small paper bag leaning against my door, the top of it rolled shut. I picked up the bag, opened the door to let in the dog, slipped off his leash, and then looked to see what was inside. A box of sugar packets. And a note:

*For you.*
*Chuck*
*P.S. Not stolen.*

I used to know a crazy woman in college who changed lifestyles the way most people change their clothes. Which is to say, more often than not. One day, you might see Janet dressed head to toe in a Sikh's outfit, complete with white turban and no makeup, and the next time you ran into her, she'd be touting Scientology and asking if you'd like to take a free personality test. I bring this up because it helps to describe the way I felt during the short period of time when I attempted to transform myself into a rock climber. Like Janet, I went all out. And also like Janet, my transformation was short-lived and maybe even crazy.

But I wanted to do it for Brian. I wanted to be the kind of girlfriend he wanted me to be: physically active and adventurous. A real rock-climbing girlfriend. All went well enough with my plan until Brian took me to do some actual rock climbing. Wasn't it sufficient that I'd purchased the teensy rubber-toed shoes, the racerback bra, the Patagonia jacket and earflap hat? Did I really have to make my way up the side of a cliff? Apparently, I did.

He started me on short climbs, nothing too steep, just enough of an incline to force me to lean into the rock wall as opposed to simply walking up the face of it. He always went first and then more or less dragged me up behind him, the rope between us taut, all the while calling out encouragement as he waited for me to finally reach the top. Try as I might, I never saw the point of it. First you are standing on the ground. Then you are standing on top of the cliff. Then you come down again. Why?

Brian decided I needed something more challenging. A real rock climb, something that would test my mettle and leave me with a feeling of accomplishment.

"Don't worry, you can handle it," he told me. "I'd never take you on something you couldn't do."

I trusted my man.

The climb he'd chosen for me didn't look too difficult from the bottom. Brian scrambled right up.

"Your turn!" he yelled down.

This will all be over in less than an hour, I told myself. I pressed my toes and fingertips into the rock and began heaving my body upward.

"See?" Brian called out. "Not so bad, huh?"

And it wasn't so bad, at least not for twenty or thirty feet or so. Then, suddenly, the going got difficult.

"I'm having a hard time," I called up to Brian.

"You're fine," Brian said. He sounded bored to death. "Keep going."

I pressed on.

"My legs are shaking," I yelled about ten minutes later.

"You can do it," he said.

"My arms are giving out!"

"You've got it made."

My arms really were giving out. I didn't have the strength to lift myself any longer. Well, so be it. Brian was going to have to lower me to the ground.

"I've had it," I said to him. "You're going to have to lower me down."

There was silence for a moment. The stark, hard silence of intense disappointment.

"I can't," he said.

"What do you mean, you can't? Just lower me."

"I can't lower you. Look down."

I looked down. Without my noticing it, the climbing route had angled up toward the right. Here the bottom of the cliff was no longer within easy reach of the length of the rope. I was up far too high to be lowered to the ground.

"Oh, my God," I said. "How am I going to get down?"

"Well, I hate to tell you this," Brian said. "But the only way down is up."

It sounded very Buddha-like: The only way down is up. Very wise. But in fact, there really was only one way down. I had to go up.

"You fucker!" I yelled.

"You can do it!"

"Fuck you! Pull me up!"

"I can't. You'll swing like a pendulum."

Again, I saw that he was right. The angle of the climb meant that if I let go, I'd swing across the face of the rock and probably knock my own nose off, a prospect Brian was finding very funny.

"Stop laughing!" I yelled at him.

"Get moving!"

"I want to go down!"

"You can do it!" he yelled to me.

Oh, how I hated him right then, even if I could relate to his annoyance with my attitude. Who likes a complainer? But could I help it if his philosophy of life was all about facing up to physical challenges, while mine ran more toward avoiding them at all costs? Of course, it really didn't matter in that moment whose philosophy was superior. It was either wrench my way to the top or dangle at the other end of Brian's rope until he let go of his end. Somehow, I wrenched my way to the top.

"Now aren't you proud of yourself?" Brian asked when I was standing next to him, looking out at the view from the edge of the cliff.

"No."

"Yes, you are."

"No, I'm not."

"Sure you are."

But I really wasn't. In fact, climbing rock walls seemed stupider than ever.

"No. Really. I'm not."

And so my brief rock-climbing career bit the dust, followed shortly by my white-water-kayaking career, my backpacking-in-the-wilderness career, and, finally, my career as Brian's future wife.

# 16

Even though I had no interest at all in such a thing, my oldest friends on earth—Gloria, Becca, and Suzanne—insisted on dragging me out for drinks in an effort to cheer me up. Nothing on earth was going to cheer me up, least of all a night out with three happily married women, but I appreciated the effort, especially since I had absolutely no other plans. And somehow, having no plans always seemed to get me in trouble. Besides, I'd known these women forever. They already knew all of my faults and all of the stupid things I'd done over the years, and they still loved me. If I spent the entire evening crying my eyes out or alternatively dancing on top of the bar, they wouldn't have blinked. You can't buy that kind of friendship.

Gloria, our resident event planner since the third grade, decided we should go to Maxwell's, which is where we used to go in college and where I hadn't been in years.

"God, this place is exactly the same as ever," Becca said after we'd squeezed our way into a table by the door.

She was right. Maxwell's had the same brick walls as always, the same long bar with stools, the same worn wood floor, the same packed-in crowd of twenty-somethings. The only difference was the decade the four of us had added to our histories. Personally, I felt pretty stupid, sucking down a Hale's at a table of old ladies, but my girlfriends didn't seem to care.

"No, it's not," Suzanne said. Suzanne is a lawyer. If there's anything to be confrontational about on any subject, she'll find it. "There's no cigarette smoke."

We all looked around, as though if we only looked hard enough, a swirl of cigarette smoke might appear.

"God, I hate progress," Becca said.

"That's because you smoke," Suzanne said.

"So do you!"

"I do not!"

"You do so!"

"Only on special occasions."

"Shut up, you guys. I want to hear about Brian," Gloria said to me. "Have you guys spoken?"

Gloria's been battling her weight since middle school, an effort that in a million years won't change the fact that she comes from a big-boned gene pool and will always be large.

"Well, actually, we had lunch," I said.

"Oh, my God! You're kidding!" Gloria said. "What happened?"

Everyone turned to look at me.

"He wants to be friends," I said.

"Fuck that," Suzanne said.

"He said he was sorry."

"What an asshole," Suzanne said.

"He said he misses me."

"Oh, God, give me a break," Suzanne said. "I hope you slapped him."

"I didn't. But I had a very nice dramatic moment where I walked out of the restaurant and left him with the bill."

"Well, I should hope so," Suzanne said.

Becca leaned forward. "You know she took all the stuff he left at her place to the dump and threw it in," she said.

"You did?" Suzanne asked.

I nodded.

"And you didn't tell me?"

"I thought you knew about that."

"I didn't. But God, that's so great! Did you really? Good for you! I need another beer! Anybody else?"

Gloria patted my hand. "We need to find you another guy," she said.

Why was that everybody's answer to everything? Why didn't anyone suggest I find enlightenment, or take a vow of poverty, or write the Great American Novel? Not that I would ever do any of those things, but couldn't someone at least suggest one of them? The fact that I needed another guy—true as it was—just sounded so pathetic.

"I don't want another guy," I said.

Gloria patted my hand more forcefully. “I know. I know,” she said.

Gloria has three children under the age of five. For several years, she’s been talking to all of us as though we’re infants. The minute she puts me in a time-out, she’s history.

“You know, I never really liked him so much,” Becca said. “I probably shouldn’t say that, but it’s true. He was kind of full of himself, you know?”

“Oh, forget him,” Suzanne said. “He had a small dick, anyway.”

We all looked at her.

“I mean, he did, didn’t he? Not that I would know or anything.”

Suzanne avoided my eyes.

“You slept with him?” I asked.

Now she looked at me.

“I didn’t!” she said.

“Yes, you did!”

“No, I didn’t!”

“Then how would you know if he had a small dick or not?”

“God, you guys!” Gloria said. “People can hear you!”

“Oh, shit,” Suzanne said. “You remember that time you broke up with him for a couple of weeks and you went out with that short guy? The Mexican?”

“He wasn’t Mexican. He was from Ecuador.”

“Whatever.”

"And I didn't go out with him. Not technically. We just had dinner."

"Right. Dinner. That's right."

"Get to the point. Brian's dick."

"Well, we sort of . . . you know . . . made out. A million years ago."

"You made out with Brian!"

"It wasn't anything!"

For a moment, I only stared at Suzanne. Then I started to laugh.

"We didn't do it!" she said. "We just got . . . sort of . . . close. And then I felt way too weird about the whole thing. I mean, it was Brian!"

"Oh, God. That is so funny!" I said.

It wasn't funny. It was horrifying. Funny-horrifying.

"Look. I don't even remember it. Really. Except that I wasn't so, you know, impressed."

"Oh, my God. And you didn't ever tell me?"

"Well, you got back together with him and . . . God! I just pretended it never happened."

Gloria patted my hand again in that maternal way of hers. Gloria can't stand confrontation.

"It's all in the past," she said.

"It wasn't small," I said.

Suzanne pursed her lips and nodded.

"It was just right."

Suzanne nodded some more. I don't know why I felt so

protective about my stupid ex-boyfriend's penis, especially seeing as how he wasn't putting it inside of me anymore.

"I need another beer," I said.

Suzanne snapped her fingers in the air. "Waitress!" she said.

"Order some food," Becca said. "I'm starving."

We drank the beers, and the three of them launched into their usual back-and-forths about kids/husbands/houses/neighbors/preschools/dinners/homework. They certainly knew how to make all of it sound entirely unappealing. Unfortunately, the carefree single life I was leading wasn't exactly appealing, either.

I had another beer. God, Suzanne almost slept with Brian? What else didn't I know? And why did I only want to chop off Brian's head and not Suzanne's?

I left my friends to their discussion and headed to the women's room, which turned out to be the size of a broom closet and almost as dark. My dad would have had a field day renovating it—a total do-over from floor to ceiling. I tried my best not to touch anything, a difficult task since the toilet dispenser was empty and I had to root around under the sink to find another roll. None. How basic is it to have toilet paper in a room with a toilet? I should have waited to pee until I got home.

Need I say there was no soap?

On the wall someone had scrawled: "Good girls go to heaven. Bad girls go everywhere else." Maxwell's needed a few more sophisticated patrons.

"Life sucks and then you die," I thought of writing, which struck me as not at all clever, but at least a lot closer to the truth.

All the next evening, Sammy's Place was deadsville. I could barely function with so little going on. It's hard to be efficient when you've got only a couple of tables to wait on instead of the usual dozen. You simply lose steam for the whole thing.

Besides, with so little to do, I couldn't stop thinking about my so-called untapped potential. I'd be thrilled as anyone to tap my potential if only I knew what potential it was I was supposed to be tapping. I was sitting in a back booth, ignoring my tables and listening to Lisa and the darling gay busboy, Tom, compare notes on bands I'd never heard of before, when suddenly Lisa kicked me under the table.

"Lover boy's back," she said to me.

"Oh, God," I said. "Not Paul again?"

Paul, my regular with the comb-over, had been in earlier in the evening and I'd served him pork chops and salad and listened to him talk about his cousin in Florida who wanted him to come visit, and maybe did I want to come along?

"Not Paul," Lisa said. "Your other lover boy."

I turned around to see Chuck talking to the hostess. He looked up and gave me a little wave.

"He's cute," Lisa said.

"I'd do him," Tom said.

"Shut up, you guys," I said.

I walked over to the booth where the hostess had placed Chuck. He was thumbing through the pages of the menu.

"You're eating here?" I asked him.

"Yes, please. What are the specials tonight?"

I rolled my eyes at him.

"How long until you get off?" he asked.

"Hold on. I'll see."

I walked back to the booth where I'd left Lisa and Tom.

"No," Lisa said.

"I didn't even ask you anything," I said.

"I'm just kidding. Yes, I'll take your tables."

"Thank you."

"But you have to call me first thing in the morning and tell me everything."

"You are so immature."

"And I mean it."

"And then you call me," Tom said to Lisa.

It was pouring rain when we walked out of the restaurant. Chuck had taken the bus to Sammy's, so we ran through the rain—me with my coat over my head in a lame attempt to forestall the inevitable hair frizz—and climbed into my car in the parking lot. My car was dog-hair city. Not only that, it now smelled very doglike, a smell that would have disgusted me in the pre–Big Guy days but which I'd quickly grown accustomed to, even sort of liked. I once had a friend who liked the smell of her own feet, even though they smelled like, well, feet. This was sort of the same thing, I supposed. Disgusting to admit, perhaps, but not out of the realm of possibility.

"Sorry my car kind of stinks," I said. "I had the Big Guy in here today and he was kind of wet."

I tried to brush some of the dog hair off the edge of the seat with the side of my hand, but it was no use. Chuck pretended not to notice.

"So, did you just need another ride home tonight or did you actually want to do something?" I asked.

"Well, speaking of the Big Guy," he said. "I thought maybe you'd want some help returning him."

"You're kidding."

"I'm not."

"Did I say I was returning him?"

"No. Not in so many words."

I didn't say anything.

"I'll help you. Come on. Picture it. The new lawful you. Clean start. Fresh slate. All of that."

"It's okay. Really."

"I'll just go up to the door and say I found him."

"No, no, no, no. I don't want you to do that. What if one day Brian sees you with Aryeh or something? He's not that stupid. He'd figure it out."

"Well, then I'll put the dog back while you drive the getaway car. It'll be very Bonnie and Clyde, but without the blood. Two minutes and you're done with it."

"I can't believe you're so concerned about that dog."

Chuck didn't say anything.

"Look, I know you're trying to be helpful and everything," I said, "but I've got it under control."

This Chuck was turning out to be a bit of a rabbi.

"Really," I said. "I can handle it."

Chuck reached up and stroked his chin as though he were pondering the great mysteries of life.

I said, "I really do appreciate your concern. Really, I do."

"You can wear a beret like Faye Dunaway."

"Okay, we'll take him back," I said.

I started up the car, and since we were closer to Brian's place than mine, Chuck suggested we drive past Brian's first so that he could calculate the difficulty level of returning the Big Guy without causing any type of disturbance—in particular the type of disturbance involving Brian emerging in a rage from the house and smashing in Chuck's skull with a baseball bat.

"It would probably be best if I could avoid bodily harm," he said to me.

"That's very practical of you," I said.

We headed to Brian's, and I asked Chuck what he'd been up to lately workwise, and he told me about the wedding he'd videotaped the week before, a wedding that had pretty much devolved into a drunken screaming match among various family members, complete with drinks tossed in faces and a brawl outside on the sidewalk.

"I get that type of thing more often than you might think," Chuck said. "And it's pretty funny, because with a little cutting and splicing, everybody's wedding looks like the happiest day of their lives."

"So people pay you to falsify information?"

"I prefer to think of it as making artistic decisions," he said.

God, if only you could really cut and splice the regrettable stuff right out of your life. Of course, in my case, there wouldn't be a whole lot of unregrettable life left over. I'd probably be something like two years old once you were finished.

"This is the street," I said as we turned onto Cascade Boulevard.

"Which one is it?"

I pointed when we got close.

"That one," I said. "The white one."

I drove past the house to the end of the block, made a U-turn, and cruised past Brian's once more. No bodies pressing against each other on the porch, thank God. No signs of life at all.

"Piece of cake," Chuck said. "Let's go get the dog."

# 17

Seriously bad news when we arrived at my apartment building: Ambulance parked at the curb. Front door wedged open. Lobby curiously empty of its usual jabbering patron saint. Carl's apartment door also wedged open. And finally, Carl himself, strapped to a gurney, his face obscured by a black mask with tubes attached, being wheeled out of his apartment door by two burly emergency workers in blue uniforms, both seemingly oblivious to the hollow grunts and groans emanating from beneath the mask of their latest patient.

"Carl!" I said.

Carl glared at me from the bottom of his deep gray eye sockets, looking like a Halloween skeleton with orbital cavities a-lit. His body on the gurney beneath the white cotton blanket tucked around him had no bulk to it whatsoever. He was all head, and that head was not happy.

"Hrrummpfff junneeenn heerrrboooddd!" he said to me.

"Excuse me?"

"*Hrrummpfff junneeenn heerrrboooooooddddd!*" he said.

"God, I'm sorry, Carl," I said. "I don't know what you're saying."

Meanwhile, the two burly emergency workers kept hauling poor Carl through the lobby and out the front door.

"What's going on?" I called after them. "Where are you taking him?"

"Viewcrest," the one nearest me said. He couldn't have sounded more bored. "He was having trouble breathing. Called 911."

"Oh."

"You know him?"

"Well, I live here. He's the super. Of the building."

"Do me a favor. Lock up his apartment."

They wheeled the gurney to the back of the ambulance, opened the ambulance doors, and slid Carl inside.

"Shouldn't I call somebody?" I asked. "A relative or something?"

"That would be good," the guy said.

And that was it. One of the burly emergency workers hopped inside next to Carl, and the other hopped into the driver's seat of the ambulance.

"Bye-bye!" said the one in the back with Carl, and he slammed the door shut just as the ambulance pulled out into the street.

"Man, that was quick," I said.

"Well, they *are* emergency workers," Chuck said.

"You think he'll be all right?"

"I don't know. He have trouble breathing before?"

"I don't know," I said. "Not that I know of."

We walked back into the building and up the entryway stairs to Carl's place.

"I've never been in there before," I said at the doorway.

Chuck took my hand. "Come on," he said. "We'll find a phone number, call a relative, and then you'll feel better."

"Okay."

Chuck pushed open the door, and I followed him inside Carl's apartment. I tiptoed. I don't know, it just seemed more appropriate to tiptoe since we hadn't really been invited in, except by the emergency workers. I wondered how the emergency workers usually handled such a situation. Shouldn't they have locked up the apartment themselves? Did they always leave the door locking to perfect strangers who happened to come upon them in the lobby? The whole thing seemed pretty flaky to me.

Carl's place smelled exactly like an old person's apartment, all heavy and putrid with used-up air. It's weird the way old people don't ever seem to open a window and let in a little fresh air. You'd think they'd get sick breathing in the same molecules over and over again. I tried not to take in too many of Carl's former air molecules, the ones he'd been breathing in and out for the last several decades, but it was impossible. I could feel the grubby little suckers zooming up my nostrils and setting up camp.

"Here," Chuck said.

Carl's phone sat on a tiny metal table just inside the kitchen. It was a beige-colored Princess phone. Or at least at one time it had been beige-colored. Now it was covered in black grime, its cord tangled hopelessly into one huge dreadlock of coil. Tacked to the wall above the phone was a yellowed paper of phone numbers and names written in tiny, illegible cursive. The paper looked as if it had been tacked to the wall since World War II.

"Can you read that?" I asked.

"There you are," Chuck said, pointing.

Sure enough, there was my name and phone number written in smudged pencil toward the bottom of the page.

"Wow," I said. "He's never called me."

"What's his last name?" Chuck said.

I thought for a moment. In nine years, I'd never known Carl's full name. I felt kind of bad about that. You'd think I would have bothered to ask.

"I don't know."

"Hmmmm." Chuck studied the list. "I think we should try one of these names at the top. They're probably relatives."

"Okay."

"You want me to do it?"

"That would be good."

Chuck called the first name on the list, a name that turned out to belong to an elderly cousin who could barely hear. After several moments of impressively patient explanation, Chuck finally got the information across.

"Okay," he said after hanging up. "He wants us to take a few things to the hospital."

"You're kidding."

"No. I'm not. He wants us to bring Carl his robe, his slippers, and his Bible."

"What did you tell him?"

"I said we'd do it."

"You did?"

"Well, sure. Of course."

"Right. Of course."

"You okay?"

I nodded. I was beginning to think maybe Chuck was the nicest person I'd ever met in my life. Offering to help me return the dog. And now offering to fetch Carl his things without even a moment's hesitation. Now he looked at me with concern on his face, and I realized my own face looked panic-stricken.

"I'll get everything, if you want," Chuck said. "You can just wait here."

"That would be good."

It sounds funny, but it seemed more okay for a stranger like Chuck to go through Carl's things than for me to do it. I mean, if Carl had ever wanted me to see his things, he would have invited me to come inside at some point over the last nine years, right? Chuck walked down Carl's hallway and took a right through a doorway.

"Bedroom!" he called out.

"Okay!" I called back.

"Got the robe!" Chuck yelled.

"Okay!"

"Slippers!"

"Okay!"

"Bingo! Bible!"

"Okay!" I called out.

Chuck emerged, holding the items in his arms.

"Ready?" he asked.

I shrugged. I was beginning to feel really bummed out. In fact, I started to cry.

"Are you crying?"

I shrugged.

"Everything's fine," Chuck said.

"Okay," I said.

If you get shot in this town, or beat up, or have a psychotic breakdown, or find yourself the victim of a really bad car accident, they take you first to Viewcrest, where the poorly lit emergency waiting room is constantly packed with bleeding, moaning people waiting to be seen. Pity the poor fool who manages to shoot himself in the hand with a nail gun at the exact same moment another poor fool manages to shoot himself in the head. The bleeding, excruciatingly painful hand injury will have to wait until the head injury is looked after, and that waiting will have to be done in the poorly lit and always jam-packed emergency waiting room.

By the time we showed up at Viewcrest, the place was

hopping. One drunk teenager, two homeless men, a kid with two broken wrists, a middle-aged woman with suspicious bruises wiping her eyes with a damp tissue while a toddler used her body for a jungle gym, a few silent couples staring at the walls, and one very old man with a bleeding forehead. Chuck walked up to the information desk and gave the heavy woman sitting behind the counter Carl's last name, which turned out to be Waverly.

"Pulmonary unit," the heavy woman said. "Sixth floor south."

Was everyone who worked in emergency services so totally bored with their jobs, or was I simply having a string of bad luck? Maybe when you dealt day after day with horrible accident victims, regular people just bored you to death.

"Which way is that?" I asked.

"You related to him?" she asked.

"No," I said. "Not really. I mean, sort of. I mean, I live in his apartment building. I'm kind of daughterly to him. Or he's fatherly. Uncleish. You know?"

"Can't go up there right now," she said.

"I can't?"

"Relatives only. Come back tomorrow. Visiting hours."

"But we have his stuff," I said. "We said we'd bring it."

"Put it here."

She tapped the counter. Then she poked through a pile of papers on her desk.

"Sparks?" she called out.

The man with the bleeding forehead stood up.

"Yes, please," I said. "If you could give him these things."

I set the robe, slippers, and Bible on the counter. The man with the bleeding forehead stepped forward. He looked ready to faint.

"Need you to sign this," the heavy woman said. She handed him a clipboard with a pen attached.

"Let's go," Chuck said.

"You'll be sure and give him these things?" I asked her.

She glanced up at me and then back down at her papers. "Perkins!" she called out.

The drunk teenager yelled, "Wha?"

"Come on," Chuck said to me. "She's got it."

"Thank you," I said to her. "We appreciate it. He really needs that stuff. So, that's just great, you taking it to him. Or being sure he gets it. Or, whatever."

"Perkins!"

"Let's go," Chuck said, taking my hand.

"What about the old deaf guy? Aren't we supposed to meet him here?"

"He just wanted us to bring Carl's things. It's fine. We can go."

I could get used to this hand-holding thing. Brian had never been a big hand-holder. He was more of a throw-his-arm-casually-over-my-shoulder-for-two-seconds kind of guy. Of course, I didn't know that for certain anymore. When Brian was my boyfriend/fiancé, I would have sworn he wasn't the kind of guy to make out on the front porch of his house, so what did I know? I wondered what else he was doing these days that he never used to do. Flower arranging? Reading to the blind? Foreplay?

Back in the car, Chuck asked if I wanted him to do the driving, but I said no, I could handle it.

"You want to go home?" he asked.

"Do you?"

Chuck looked at his bare wrist as though he might find a watch there.

"We could still return the dog," he said. "It's early yet."

The dog. Chuck really wanted me to get rid of the dog. Well, all right already. I'd get rid of the dog.

The Big Guy was deliriously happy to see me, so much so that he peed on my leg while jumping up to say hello.

"Time to go home, buddy," I said to him.

My throat tightened up when I said it. I reminded myself that it hadn't been so very long ago that I didn't even know the Big Guy existed, and also that chances were excellent Carl would be back manning his post in the alcove in the very near future. Things would be normal again. Still, I had to rip a few squares of toilet paper from the bathroom roll to wipe the tears from my face and blow my nose before continuing with the plan.

Chuck was waiting for the two of us in my car. I took the Big Guy by his purple collar, grabbed his favorite of all my socks for him to chew on during the ride to Brian's, and headed back down the stairs. And although the alcove was always empty late at night—Carl had always sacked out by eleven P.M. at the very latest—it still seemed emptier than usual when we walked through.

"Okay, let's get our plan straight," Chuck said when the dog and I were in the car.

"Right."

"You pull over in front of the house. I put the dog back in his pen. I get back in the car. You pull away."

"Better go over that again."

Chuck smiled. We drove for a moment in silence.

"You doing okay?" Chuck asked.

"Yeah."

"I don't know. You seem kind of attached to that dog and everything."

"I do?"

"You do."

"I guess I am, sort of."

"You can always get another one."

"No, I can't. Not in my building."

"Oh. Right."

"But I should move anyway."

"Why's that?"

"God, I've been there forever. It's time."

Chuck nodded.

"Okay, if the lights are on inside of the house, we cancel," I said.

"Okay," Chuck said.

"And if we see any neighbors outside, that cancels, too."

"Okay."

"And if he starts barking, then just be very, very fast."

"Got it."

I put a hand over the top of the seat and reached back to pat the Big Guy.

"You drove me crazy, but you were all right," I said to him. "And sorry for stealing you."

"He forgives you," Chuck said.

Why was this Chuck such a nice guy? He was the exact opposite of me. Emotionally stable. Able to see the big picture. Grounded. Just plain nice.

"You are so nice," I said to him.

I've always had a difficult time editing my thoughts. Any random spark floating around my brain has an excellent chance of revealing itself to whoever is in the vicinity. This, I might add, is not one of my better attributes.

"Thanks," Chuck said. "So are you."

"No, I'm not. I stole a dog."

Chuck shook his head. "Temporary insanity," he said. "Happens to the best of us."

"Did you have a perfect childhood or something? Is that why you're so grounded?"

Chuck laughed. "Who has the perfect childhood? Come on. Mine was as fucked up as anyone's. Why do you think I moved three thousand miles away?"

"Yeah. Why did you?"

Chuck shrugged. "Change is good," he said.

"I hate change."

"Yeah. But it's still good."

"Yeah. I guess."

"Also. Everything kept reminding me of Glenda Waters. It seemed like a good idea to get out of town."

"Oh," I said. "So you still have a thing for Glenda Waters?"

Chuck shrugged. "Not really," he said. "Sort of. I don't know."

"Sorry."

"It's okay. Change is good."

"Right. Change is very, very good."

"Change is fucking excellent."

"Party on, Wayne!"

I took a right up Cascade Avenue and slowed the car to a creep. From a distance, all looked quiet.

"So far, so good," I whispered.

"Good thing you're whispering," Chuck whispered.

"Shut up," I whispered.

"You're very pretty when you're angry," Chuck whispered.

I stopped in front of Brian's house. No lights on.

"The coast is clear," I whispered.

Chuck stepped out into the darkness, opened the back door, and let the Big Guy leap out.

"Be right back," he said.

"Hold on a second," I said.

I cut the engine and got out of the car.

"Come here, you," I said to the dog.

I leaned over, and the Big Guy padded over to me and licked my face.

"Brian doesn't deserve you," I said.

"Okay," Chuck said. "Come on. Let's do this thing."

I stood up. Somewhere in the distance a dog barked. The Big Guy's ears popped up.

"Okay," I said.

I looked at Chuck, and in that instant the Big Guy took off, barking and flying down the street and into the darkness.

Confession: I have always gone for the strong, silent type. Take Brian, for instance. He had the strong part down to a science. He was one strong guy. Very muscled. Very six-packish. Very low in the fat department. And you know what? I'll admit it. I always liked that about him. I liked the fact that he kept his body in such fabulous condition, even if it meant he spent an ungodly amount of time working out to keep his body in that fabulous condition.

And silent? Brian had that one pretty much wrapped up, too. If only they gave a medal for keeping thoughts and feelings hidden under the world's most shatterproof cone of silence, Brian would be the Lance Armstrong of suppression. Of course, the silent part of Brian was always far less attractive than the strong part, but since they came together in one single package, and since I'm incredibly shallow, I was willing to overlook his total lack of communicative skill.

Being in love with Brian, therefore, was no walk in the

park. This fact was something I attempted to remember whenever possible. Unfortunately, I have a terrible memory. Or I have a fantastic memory, but only for the good stuff. Like Brian's six-pack. God, shallow, shallow, shallow. And completely unfair of me to wonder if Chuck had a six-pack or even a four-pack beneath that perennially wrinkled blue shirt of his. Utterly unfair and ridiculous to wonder if a guy with a sense of humor and a bit of tenacity could also, miraculously, be an all right guy in bed.

As it turned out, I'd have to continue wondering. After wandering the blocks around Brian's house for over an hour and then driving over the same territory—both times coming up empty—Chuck needed to get home.

"I'm sorry," he said. "But you know, I don't think we're going to find that dog tonight. And it's getting pretty late."

"Oh," I said.

I tried to sound both disappointed and not disappointed at the same time, which only managed to cancel out both attempts.

"Tomorrow, we can call the pound," he said.

"Okay."

"And to tell you the truth, I've actually got company," he said. "My cousin's here from New Jersey. Part of a little West Coast swing he's making to drive my aunt crazy before he starts college in January."

"Oh," I said.

"Chances are excellent he's poking through my stuff and stealing all the good DVDs."

"Oh. Right. Okay."

As we drove through the mostly deserted streets, I wondered if Chuck would try to kiss me when I dropped him off, and what kind of a kiss it might be, and what level of enthusiasm I should display in response to his kiss, which of course depended on what kind of kiss he offered. But maybe it was too early to be thinking about a response, seeing as how that would imply a kiss was imminent, and I couldn't be altogether certain of such a thing. Or could I? Of course he wanted to kiss me. What was I thinking?

Fortunately, before I could do any more wondering, we were on his block and Chuck was saying, You can pull over right here. So I pulled over to the curb.

"You going to be all right?" Chuck asked.

"Sure," I said.

"Okay." He hopped out of the car, then leaned his face in again. "You made a very good Bonnie."

At that, he slammed the door shut and disappeared into his building.

# 18

I didn't sleep. In the morning, I called the pound. A man on the other end with a very loud and awfully cheerful voice told me, yes, they did have a couple of yellow labradors on the premises, but neither of them had been brought in during the last twenty-four hours! Sorry!

"Well, can I leave you my number so you can call me if another yellow lab is turned in?"

"Sure thing!" the happy employee shouted, as though I had just made his day with my request.

Ten seconds later, my phone rang.

"That was quick!" I said.

"What was quick?" my dad said.

"Oh. I thought you were someone else."

"Don't sound so disappointed."

"No, no. I'm not. Come on. Of course not. It's just that . . . Well, it's just that . . . I managed to sort of . . . lose the Big

Guy last night, and I was hoping that was the pound calling me back to say they'd found him."

"You *lost* your dog?"

"Yeah."

"How does a person lose a dog?"

"Yeah. Well. I'm about to head out now. Go find him. I think I know where he is."

I didn't know what I was saying. There was no way I was going to find that dog. I'd already searched everywhere. I felt like killing myself for spilling the beans to my dad. If only I weren't so tired.

"Okay. Gosh, I hope you find it. That was a nice dog. Anyway, I was just calling to see if you're going to this mystery dinner your mother is having."

"Mystery dinner? You mean Sunday night?"

"That's the one."

"Yeah. I'll be there."

"Well, all right, then, I'll see you then."

After we hung up, I started to wonder if Alicia was going to show up on Sunday without the wig. Or maybe she'd already put it back on. Maybe the no-wig moment had passed. I gave her a call.

"Can you talk?" I asked when she picked up the phone.

"Not really."

"Not really, like Aryeh's standing there? Or not really, like you don't feel like talking?"

"The first one."

"Oh. Okay. But did you put your wig back on?"

"You know what? I'll call you back, how's that?"

And she hung up.

Then I called Chuck to tell him the Big Guy hadn't been brought to the pound.

"He'll turn up," Chuck said.

Then he excused himself to get back to burning a pile of CDs for his cousin.

I spent the rest of the morning studying the pages of an old issue of *People,* mostly staring at a spread of photos of Angelina Jolie and wondering how it was possible for one person to have been born with all perfect body parts at once, and then wondering if Chuck's old girlfriend Glenda Waters had perfect body parts, and then wondering if it would be a problem if he ever saw me naked and found out my body parts were slightly less than perfect, but finally deciding that anyone not legally blind would already know my body wasn't perfect just from seeing it in clothes, meaning that Chuck already knew, sort of. Or maybe he didn't. Or maybe he didn't mind. He was an artist, wasn't he? Maybe he liked bodies that were original. But he didn't want to sleep with me, anyway. He hadn't even kissed me. But maybe he did. Maybe he just was the type of guy who moved very, very slowly. But if he did sleep with me, then he'd see my body, which wasn't perfect, the way his old girlfriend's probably was. I continued in this circular and completely shallow line of thought until finally Lisa called and tried to convince me to come along to her yoga class.

"You need to breathe," she said to me.

"I am breathing."

"You're not. You're inhaling. But you're not breathing."

I'd tried yoga before. Twice. And both times I couldn't for the life of me understand how anyone could possibly find such torturous exercise enjoyable. The first class—taught by a ninety-pound brunette bulldog in a unitard—left me with a miserable headache and the kind of body ache you'd normally associate with a particularly virulent form of the flu. The second class was led by a sixty-plus-year-old hippie with streaming gray hair and a slight potbelly. Although I prayed she wouldn't, she did indeed request that class members touch each other's feet, after which I didn't breathe for the remainder of the class.

"Maybe some other time," I said.

"You'll never go, will you?" Lisa asked.

"Probably not."

"Then let's eat."

We met at Lily's, a coffee shop near Green Lake famous for serving huge platters of food to customers who mostly look as though they've already had a few platters too many. I found Lisa sitting in a booth in the back, wearing sunglasses and one of her yoga outfits: skinny black pants of some sort of stretchy material, tiny white T-shirt, hair pulled back and held in place with a thick headband.

"Good morning, Audrey Hepburn," I said.

"Oh, yeah," she said, and took off the sunglasses. "I thought it was kind of dark in here."

The incredibly bored and fabulously pierced waitress

thunked down our coffee mugs, took our orders without once taking a glance at either of us, and then disappeared. About a minute later, she returned with our plates of eggs and home fries.

"That was fast," Lisa said, smiling at her.

She walked away.

"I'm leaving her a huge tip," I said. "She's brilliant."

We dug into our plates of food, and I listened while Lisa complained about the way her boyfriend kept losing money playing online poker and about how he spent so much time online that he didn't even come to bed anymore and how if he didn't get over this gambling thing pretty soon, she was going to lose patience and tell him to move out.

"Tell him to move out now. I need at least one friend without a husband or a boyfriend," I said.

"Speaking of which," she said. "What's the latest with Brian's dog?"

"I was hoping you wouldn't ask."

"You killed him?"

"I lost him," I said.

"You what?"

"I lost him, all right? I'm a terrible person. I didn't mean to lose him. I meant to take him back. But he ran away and now I don't know where he is."

"Start from the top."

"Okay. Chuck and I were returning him—God, last night was the longest night—and right when we got out of the car the dog just . . . ran off. Like that. And we drove around looking for him, but he never turned up. So I suck. I lost Brian's dog, and now my whole life is just a wreck."

"What are you going to do?"

"What *can* I do?"

Oh, God, I didn't want to start crying right there in the diner, but I couldn't help myself. I'm an idiot.

"Can I borrow your sunglasses?" I asked Lisa.

She handed them over, set down her fork, leaned back in her chair, and looked at me while I told her the part about Carl and the hospital and about dropping Chuck off at his apartment after losing the dog.

"Wait a second. Back up. Are you telling me you didn't sleep with him?"

"I didn't sleep with him."

Lisa stared at me. "You didn't sleep with Chuck? Why didn't you?"

"What do you mean, why didn't I?"

"I mean, why didn't you?"

"One guess."

Lisa's eyes went wide. "He didn't want to?" she asked.

I didn't say anything.

"Wow. You really need to get laid."

"Shut up. My psyche is not dependent on whether or not I get laid," I said.

"Sure it is. God."

I slathered a piece of toast with a big wad of butter, all the while telling myself inside my head that eating toast covered with that much butter was a really stupid thing to do, and not just weightwise, but healthwise. Then I ate the whole thing.

"Well, I don't have any prospects," I said.

"Don't even think in terms of prospects. Men are horny. They'll fuck anything. Really. You've got your pick of the lot."

"What a refreshing way to look at things."

"Look around. Any one of these guys would happily sleep with you in a heartbeat."

We looked around. In the far corner, a fat man in baggy gray trousers and an alarming series of chins was making a very large dent in his platter of eggs and home fries. Two gay men sat on stools at the corner, looking very cute and very gay. In the booth behind us, four teenage girls in black makeup and various dye jobs drank coffee and made faces at one another.

"Great," I said.

"Well, you know what I mean."

"Look, I know it's an old-fashioned concept, but I really don't want to fuck just anybody."

"No one said you had to fuck just anybody. We'll find you a nice-looking guy. You'll see."

"You are so shallow."

Lisa poured a steady stream of ketchup all over her home fries. "Look. I'm taking you to a bar. And you're going to meet a guy. And you're going to take him home, all right? God, you'd think it was difficult or something."

"Maybe."

"Maybe shmaybe."

On the way home, I gave myself fifty points for not driving past Brian's house.

I was back at my apartment, staring at the Big Guy's water bowl and picturing the Big Guy lost and alone in the universe—shivering in a dark alley, moaning with hunger, his purple collar tattered and soaked with grime—when the phone rang. I looked at my cell's screen to see the number. Unknown. Breaking my own cardinal rule, I picked up.

"Rena?" Mr. Benning said.

"Mr. Benning?"

"Yes. It's me. Tom. I hope I'm not bothering you?"

"Oh, no. No problem. How are you?"

"Have you got a minute, dear?" Mr. Benning asked.

"Sure. Yeah. Of course."

"I won't keep you long."

"That's okay. What's up?"

"Well, in fact, I'm in town. I thought maybe you might let me buy you dinner."

I pulled the phone from my ear and looked at it. Was Mr. Benning asking me out on a date? No, that couldn't be it. He just . . . missed me, that was all. And in a strange way, I sort of missed him, too. But not enough to have dinner with him.

"Oh. You mean, like, tonight? Gosh, I'm sorry, I'm all booked up. Gee, that's too bad. But maybe next time."

"Oh, well. Okay, then. Next time."

"I'm sure I'll be free next time."

"Well, there's one more thing."

"Sure. What is it?" I asked.

"Well, dear," Mr. Benning said, "I'm actually looking at a picture of you right now."

Oh, God. What picture of me was he looking at?

"Yeah?" I said.

"And it seems you've lost a dog."

"Excuse me?"

"Well, I'm looking at a photo of you holding on to what looks like, I don't know, a yellow labrador? Anyway, it says: 'Lost Dog. Reward for return.' And then there's your phone number. Which is how I got your phone number, by the way."

*"What?"*

"It's a poster, dear. You know, a flyer. On a telephone pole."

I tried to stay calm. Al must have taken the photo he'd snapped of me and the Big Guy at Green Lake and made a few "Lost Dog" signs.

"Where exactly are you standing, Mr. Benning?"

"Let's see. Corner of Madrona and Forty-seventh."

Madrona and 47th. About five or six blocks away from my apartment.

"Wow. That's weird. Hmmm. Well, I did lose a dog, sort of. It's a long story."

"You mean it was stolen? Because it's strange, really, but Brian and Anna's dog—it was a yellow labrador, too—it was stolen a few days ago. Maybe someone's stealing yellow labradors."

"No, no. Not stolen. Not mine. Lost. Definitely lost. Wow, that's weird about Brian and Anna's, though."

"Yes. Well. Is there anything I can do?"

"You? Wow, thanks for asking. But no. I don't think there's anything you can do. But I appreciate you letting me know. About the flyer. Gosh, that was nice of somebody! Look, I better go. Thanks for calling. We'll have dinner. Next time I'm in Portland. I promise!"

I hung up the phone, rang up Lisa, and together we spent the next three hours scouring the streets of my neighborhood for flyers and tearing them down. My dad had been a very busy guy. He must have hit every telephone pole within a fifteen-block radius. Finally, we seemed to have gotten them all.

"Okay," Lisa said to me. "I hope this whole stupid dog thing is over."

"God, me too," I said.

After which I called my dad to thank him.

# 19

When Brian called the next day three times in one hour and left voice mails each time asking me to please call him back, I got nervous. Maybe I'd missed one of the flyers my dad had put up and he'd seen it. Maybe he'd known all along that I'd taken the Big Guy and now he was calling to ream me out for losing him instead of bringing him back. Or maybe not. Maybe he'd finally come to the realization that a short, slightly fleshy Jewish girl was vastly superior to a perfectly proportioned blond Amazon.

Whatever the reason, I decided he was going to have to call a fourth time to finally get through to me. Which he did, a few moments later.

"Oh, good," he said. "You answered."

"What's going on?"

"Listen. Do you have a moment? Where are you?"

"Where are *you*? On the sidewalk in front of my apartment?"

"No, but I can be."

"What do you want, Brian?"

"Nothing, really. Can I come over?"

"No, you can't come over. What do you want?"

"Just let me come over."

"If you have something to tell me, just say it now."

If he was going to scream at me about the Big Guy, there was no sense letting him do so in person. Brian hesitated for a moment.

"Look. Anna's out of town until next week," he said. "She's at her parents' in Montana."

"And I need Anna's travel itinerary for some reason?"

"It's just that I've been thinking about you."

"What do you mean, you've been thinking about me?"

"You know. Thinking about you, thinking about you."

"That's not really specific enough."

"The thing is . . . I want to see you."

"God, Brian."

"I love you. I don't know. I just do."

"That is so stupid to say to me. You live with somebody else, you asshole."

"If you'd just let me see you."

"You are a terrible boyfriend."

"Rena, please. Let me come over. I won't stay. I promise."

"You can't come over."

"Why not?"

"Because," I said.

"You met somebody?"

"Leave me alone," I said.

"God," Brian said.

"I'm going now."

"Who? It's not Derrick, is it? Please don't tell me you're sleeping with Derrick."

"Who I'm sleeping with is none of your business."

"Shit. God, I can't believe this."

"Look, I've got to go, okay? This isn't a good time."

"I still want to see you."

"Gotta go, Brian," I said.

I thought about the phone call for the rest of the day. The fact that Brian had called me the very moment Anna went out of town could only mean one of three things.

One: He was a total and complete asshole with a tendency to step out on girlfriends, which in that case meant that he had most likely stepped out on me without my knowledge at some point during his seven-year tenure with yours truly.

Two: He wanted me back.

Three: All of the above.

Whichever it was, it didn't particularly matter. He couldn't walk out on me the moment we decided to get engaged, move in with someone else, acquire a *dog* with that someone else, and then expect me to simply leap back into his arms the moment that someone else went out of town. No, he was going to have to suffer first. He was going to have to live in the deep, dark pit he'd dug for himself, swallow the bitter bile of abandonment. He was going to have to beg.

And then, I'd leap.

---

I went to work that night, and even though I really didn't expect Chuck to show up at Sammy's Place, I couldn't help but hope he would. Life had suddenly become a lot more interesting since Chuck showed up to complicate things. All through my shift, I kept checking the front door for him. Each time I went to the kitchen, I imagined it possible that I'd pop back out through the kitchen doors and there he'd be, sitting in one of my booths, wearing a wrinkled shirt, and saying something clever.

But it didn't happen. Now that we were finished with the dog, he'd lost all interest in me.

"What's with you tonight?" Lisa asked.

"Nothing."

"Well, table six is getting just a wee bit antsy."

I looked over at table six, where a man and woman in their sixties were trying to catch somebody's eye, their faces unmistakably clenched with rising anger.

"I have table six?"

"You have table six. Also seven, eight, and nine."

"Got it."

The clenched-face couple was gathering up their things to leave. I looked at Lisa and shrugged.

"I don't have the energy for this anymore," I said.

"Yeah, I'm thinking of giving notice, too."

"Did I say I'm thinking of giving notice?"

"I think so. I think that's what it means when you say you don't have the energy for this anymore."

I nodded.

"If we give notice, what will we do?" I asked.

Lisa laughed as though I'd just told her a good one.

"Well, duh," she said. "We'll find other jobs."

Sunday evening, I showed up at my mother's promptly at seven to find my father and Ron already there, sitting across from each other in the living room and searching desperately for something to talk about.

"Oh! She's here!" my father shouted when he saw me. He leapt to his feet, clearly relieved by my appearance.

"Let the party begin!" I said.

"Hello, Rena," Ron said, standing. "How's everything?"

"Give us a hug!" Al shouted. He wrapped his arms around me as though we hadn't seen each other in a decade. In his dark brown shirt buttoned to the neck and neatly combed hair, he had the distinct aura of a kid forced to dress up to go to church. His chin looked pretty well beaten up by his razor.

"Hi, Dad," I said. "Hi, Ron. I'm good. How about you?"

Ron nodded. "Good, good," he said.

"That's good," I said.

"Okay, then," my dad said.

"Okay!" I said.

"All right," Ron said.

The three of us stood uncomfortably for a moment in the middle of my mother's cluttered living room, which smelled strongly of the powder she loves to sprinkle over her carpets before vacuuming. My mother doesn't believe anything is really clean unless it smells of a cleaning product.

"Well, sit down, you two," I said.

My father and Ron both took a seat. That's when I noticed that Ron wasn't wearing his glasses. This sudden absence of his trademark accessory threw me for a loop. It was as if someone had cut off his nose.

"Ron," I said, "you get contacts?"

"I did," he said.

"Nice," I said. "You look very nice that way. I mean, you look nice with glasses, too, of course. But the contacts. It's a nice change."

"Thank you."

No one said anything for a moment. My dad was finding one of the little boxes from India that had sat on the coffee table for as long as I could remember extremely interesting. He picked it up and studied it from different angles. He opened it up and looked inside, then took his finger and swept around the bottom of it as though searching for clues to a murder.

"Where's Alicia?" I asked.

"Couldn't make it," Ron said. "Two of her kids were throwing up."

I nodded. I wondered if it was true. More likely she was having another wig breakdown or a fight with Aryeh. I wished she would call and catch me up on things.

"That's too bad," I said.

"Yes. Yes, it is," my dad said. "But you know kids. They throw up!"

"They sure do!" Ron said.

"What about Mom?" I asked.

"In the kitchen," they both said at once.

"I guess I'll go see if she needs help," I said.

At that, Ron leapt to his feet.

"Oh, no, you make yourself comfortable. I'll assist Helen," he said, and dashed out of the living room before anyone could voice a protest, leaving a trail of musty cologne in his wake.

"I'll assist Helen," my dad said in a mocking, squeaky voice.

"Dad," I said.

"Oh, for Christ's sake, she doesn't need any help. Twenty-nine years I never had to help her."

I didn't say anything in response to this confession. Why point out the obvious?

"I'm sorry, darling," he said. "How are you?"

"Fine. Okay. No, I'm good. Really."

"I wasn't arguing."

"Well, I was just being complete."

"You find that dog yet?"

"No. Didn't find the dog."

My dad nodded. "How's that Chaim fellow?" he asked.

"That Chaim fellow is probably fine. I wouldn't know."

"Your mother said you were dating him! What happened?"

"Well, my mother had it wrong. We're not dating. We weren't dating. There was nothing between us at all."

"Oh, sorry."

"No, it's fine. I'm good. Who needs a boyfriend? Ha! I'm really, really good."

"Good. I'm glad you're good. I'm terrible."

"You're what?"

"Oh, Christ. I'm not an idiot. I know why she invited me here. She's going to move in with the guy. Or marry him. Or have his baby. I don't know. Something."

"Marriage. She's going to marry him."

My dad looked at me. For the slightest moment, his eyes welled up. Then he shook his head and returned to normal.

"Fine," he said. "I can handle it. I've got a little something up my sleeve, too, you know."

"What do you mean by that?"

"I met somebody," he said.

"You what?"

"I met somebody. You know. A woman. She's in the plumbing business. My plumbing business."

I couldn't believe he hadn't given me this tidbit of information the other day on our walk. Unfortunately, I didn't have a chance to interrogate him because just then my mother called us all to the table for dinner. She broke the news of her engagement after serving up meat loaf and mashed potatoes, and I was very glad I'd told my dad in advance so that he didn't have to go through the eye-welling moment in front of my mother and Ron. Instead, he took the news in stride, even so much as lifting a glass of wine in toast to the new couple. But as soon as dinner ended, he professed to having a sore stomach and took off.

"Well," my mother said. "That went much better than I expected."

When I got home, I called my dad to pump him for more information. I didn't want details. It was bad enough to think of my mother and Ron in a carnal lock. The idea of Al having sex . . . well, there would be no ideas about Al, carnal or otherwise. I only wanted to know how the whole thing had come about and where it might be headed. I only wanted to know if it was truly possible that both of my parents had found success in the romance arena, and if so, why hadn't those particular genes been passed along to me. Had I been adopted, perhaps, and no one had ever bothered to tell me?

"Tell all," I said to my dad when he picked up.

"She's fifty-one. Floor manager in the showroom. Short. Big smiler. Very funny. I think you'll like her. Melanie. That's her name. Melanie Strauss. Nice Jewish girl."

"Fifty-one?"

My dad was sixty-two.

"I'm very youthful."

"God. Fifty-one. Has she been married before?"

"Twice."

"Kids?"

"Two. Boys. Both in college."

"Wow."

"What's wow?"

"I don't know. You. Her. Two boys in college."

"Listen. She's very sweet. You'll like her."

"Oh, God! You're not marrying her!"

"No, no. We just met."

"Good. No popping the question just to get back at Mom."

"Wouldn't do that. But for crying out loud, I don't know what she sees in that guy."

We talked a little bit longer about Melanie and then he said, Speak of the devil, because she was beeping him on the other line.

"Later, hon," he said to me.

It was early yet. I was just about to call Alicia to see if the story about the throwing-up kids was true when my mother called. In truth, I'd been expecting her. My mother always likes to replay social events over the phone.

"So," my mother said. "Pretty good, huh? It went well?"

"It went just fine, Ma."

"Yes, it did. It really did. I'm so relieved."

"I'm glad you're relieved."

"Well, I am."

"That's good."

"Yes, it is."

"I think we've covered that now."

"I don't know. We could probably go over that again."

"Let's not."

"Say, you haven't heard from Alicia, have you?" my mother asked.

"No. Why?"

"Oh, nothing."

"What? What is it?"

My mother can't keep a secret to save her life.

"It's nothing. Why? Do *you* know something?" she asked me.

"No."

"You don't?"

"No, I don't. Is there something to know?"

"Well, don't say anything."

"I won't."

"Promise. God. I don't want to get in trouble."

"I won't say anything. I promise."

"She stopped wearing her wig."

"I know."

"You know?"

"She came over."

"You knew and you didn't tell me?"

"Mother."

"What do you make of the whole thing?"

"I don't know. I think she just got tired of the wig."

"God, I've never liked that wig business—nowhere in the Torah does it say anything about a wig!—but I hope they're not breaking up. Do you think they're breaking up?"

"Aryeh and Alicia? No. They're not breaking up. I don't think they are. I don't know. Are they breaking up?"

"Can't anyone stay together anymore?"

"Ma! You started it!"

"I didn't start anything."

"You split up with Dad!"

"Your father left me."

"You wanted him to go."

"Well, I'm happy now."

"Good for you."

"Good for me."

"How did we get on to this?"

"It doesn't matter. I want you to be happy, too."

"Let's get back to Alicia."

"I want you to be happy. I can't help it. You know, you have kids and all you want is for them to eat, sleep, and be happy. And you can't get them to do any of them! Have you ever tried to get a kid to go to sleep? Or to eat something? It's impossible! How can you make your kid be happy?"

"You can't."

"No, you can't."

"You can't make anyone happy."

"No, you can't."

"It's so hard."

I could hear my mother start to sniffle on the other end of the line.

"And it's the people you love," she said. "It's not fair. You should be able to make someone else be happy if you love them. But you can't!"

"Mom, are you crying?"

"Just a little."

"I'm sorry."

"Don't be sorry that your mother only wants you to be happy!"

I didn't mean to. But hearing my mother cry—I sort of choked up, too.

"Are you crying?" my mother asked.

"Yeah. A little bit."

I could hear my mother blowing her nose.

"This is nice," she said when she came back on. "You crying, and me crying. This is nice. We're bonding!"

"God, don't ruin it."

"I'm not ruining anything."

"Ma. I'm hanging up now."

"No, I'm hanging up now."

"Good."

"Call me."

"I don't have to. You always call me," I said.

But my mother was already gone.

# 20

Carl still wasn't back. It seemed awfully strange not to find him in the alcove, cackling his old-man laugh and running off on some subject or another that no one had brought up in the first place. There had been times in the past, of course, when I'd walked through the alcove and he hadn't been there. But this time was different. This time I knew he wasn't inside his apartment heating up a TV dinner or down in the laundry room clearing lint from the screen of the dryer. No, he was in a hospital bed at Viewcrest, and if I were a nicer person, I'd go visit him there and ease his mind about the state of the alcove in his absence.

I was walking past the closed door of Carl's apartment Monday morning, on my way out to get a coffee, when all at once the door opened and a man I'd never seen before stepped through, an older man with cropped gray hair and glasses and a somewhat concave face, as though someone had turned his skull inside out and back again but failed to punch it back all the way.

"Hello," I said to him.

"Hello," he said.

"Can I help you?" I said.

It was a weird thing to say, I'll admit. But I felt protective of the building in general and of Carl's apartment in particular. Who was this interloper I'd never seen before, walking out of Carl's door as though it were his own?

"You looking for . . . Mr. Waverly?" I asked.

"I'm his son."

"Oh. His son. I didn't know he had a son. Oh. I'm sorry."

The man nodded again.

"You're his son," I said like an idiot.

"Yes."

"How's he doing?" I asked. "I mean, I was here when they took him to the hospital. In fact, we brought some of his things there. My friend and I did."

"Oh, that was very nice of you. Thank you."

"So, how's he doing?"

"Actually, he died."

I couldn't help it. I jumped at the news. It was that surprising, like someone had come up from behind and poked me in the waist, making me jump.

"What?" I said.

"Early this morning."

"No."

"I'm afraid so."

"Oh, God. I'm so sorry."

Carl's son nodded. "He was eighty-eight, you know," he said.

"Oh. Yeah."

"His body just gave out."

"Wow. Yeah. Gosh. I'm sorry."

"Thank you."

"Wow. I'm just really surprised."

The man smiled at me, and I could see his gums and they were a flaming pink, just like Carl's.

"Your dad was a nice man," I said.

"Thank you," he said. "I appreciate that."

I wondered if I should tell him more—like how his dad hung out in the alcove a lot, talking everyone's ear off, and how we all sort of liked that about him, how we sort of counted on him being there—but the son was turning to lock Carl's door, and it seemed the moment had passed.

The son turned around.

"Are you by any chance Rena?" he asked me.

"Rena?" I said. "I mean, yes. Yes, I am."

I hoped we hadn't disturbed anything in Carl's apartment when we retrieved his things.

"The hamburger-and-French-fries Rena?"

"Oh. Yeah. That would be me."

"He told me about you."

"He did?"

"It was real nice of you to do that."

"It wasn't anything."

"Yes, it was. To my dad it was, anyway."

He smiled at me. "Well, you take care now," he said.

I watched him leave, and as the front door to the building fell shut again, I couldn't help but notice the NO DOGS ALLOWED sign still affixed to it. I didn't want to look at that sign anymore. I took it down from the front door, but then I didn't know what to do with it, so I put it back up.

All day long, everything felt weird. I kept forgetting Carl was dead and then remembering again and then feeling bad about forgetting. Finally, I decided to call Chuck and give him the news.

"No," Chuck said. "God, that's too bad."

In truth, I was pleased to have an excuse to talk to him, although a different kind of excuse would have pleased me more.

"Yeah," I said.

"Well, maybe he had a great life."

"Maybe."

"And it was long, anyway."

"Yeah."

"Are you okay?" Chuck asked.

"Yeah. I'm okay. It's a little weird, I guess."

"Well, he was pretty much a part of your daily existence for quite a few years."

"That's true."

"Every time you came down those stairs, practically."

"Yeah."

We didn't talk for a moment.

"Any news on the Big Guy?" Chuck asked.

"Nothing. I've called the pound a hundred times."

"Too bad."

"Yeah."

There was silence again. Uncomfortable silence. Then, finally, Chuck spoke.

"Do you want me to come over?"

"Would you?"

"I've got a couple of things I have to do, but then I'll be there."

I made a valiant attempt to straighten my apartment, mostly by tossing as much as possible into my closet and closing the closet door. Still, the place was a mess. God, did I need to get a grip. I didn't need a therapist to tell me there was something psychologically screwy about a person willing to live in such chaos. Just as I was filling the sink with soapy water to wash the dirty dishes that had graced my counter for who knew how many days, Chuck appeared.

"Wait," he said. "I've got to film this."

"Hey," I said, shutting off the water. "Thanks for coming over."

"No problem."

We looked at each other for a moment. Chuck had exchanged his usual wrinkled button-down shirt for a wrinkled black T-shirt that had the word *Brooklyn* printed on it in very faded white letters. Now that he'd come over, I didn't know what to say.

"You thirsty?" I asked like an idiot. "I'd offer you some coffee, but . . ."

"I don't need coffee," he said. "Unless you do."

"I'm fine."

"Let me help you with those dishes."

"God, no!" I said. "Forget the dishes."

"No, really," he said. "It looks kind of fun."

Chuck turned on the faucet again, and together we watched the soap bubbles rise into a small mountain. It was nice just to stand so close to him. He smelled good.

"What is that smell?" I asked him. "Some kind of cologne or something?"

"Soap," he said. "Or shampoo. I don't know. I just took a shower."

"I should try that sometime."

He smiled. Then he leaned toward me and put his nose into my hair. My whole body prickled at the slight brush of his nose against my scalp.

"It's nice," he said, pulling away. "Whatever you use."

I plunged both my hands into the water to stop myself from doing something stupid, like grabbing Chuck and ripping off all of his clothes. He was so confusing. I felt like a teenager, wondering what was going on and being nervous in his company. He put a pile of dishes into the sink, plucked a plate from the water, and began scrubbing at it with a sponge.

"You dry," he said.

He handed me the plate and went back to his scrubbing, and I picked up a towel and dried the plate, and the two of us went on like that for a few minutes without talking. It was very pleasant to have someone there and not have to speak to them. Brian and I had been like that once, but that seemed like a long, long time ago.

"So, it's been quite the week," Chuck said finally.

"Yeah," I said.

"I feel really bad about the Big Guy. About losing him, I mean."

"It wasn't your fault."

"It was, sort of. I should have had him on the leash."

"Well, if I hadn't stolen him in the first place . . ."

"Well, if your old boyfriend had never gotten that dog in the first place," he said. He held up another plate for me to dry.

"Anna."

"What?"

"It's her dog. The new girlfriend's."

"Oh. Right."

I dried the plate and waited for another.

"My sister took off her wig," I told him.

"She what?"

"My sister decided to stop wearing her wig."

"Wow. What happened?"

"She just didn't want to wear it anymore."

"I can't believe it. That's huge."

"And my mother's getting married," I said. "To Ron."

"You are just full of news."

"And my dad has a girlfriend."

Chuck stopped scrubbing and looked at me, his hands still in the soapy water.

"I can't take any more," he said.

"There isn't any more."

"Phew."

"Except I'm pretty sure I'm going to quit my job."

"You're kidding."

"No. I can't work there anymore. I just can't."

"What are you going to do?"

"I don't know. God, I really do not know. All I know is that if I spend one more day at that restaurant, I'm going to have to kill myself."

Chuck finished scrubbing another plate and handed it to me to dry, but somehow it slipped through my fingers, and the plate—it happened to be my favorite, a pretty blue one with a ring of yellow flowers around the edge that Brian had once bought for me in a thrift store in Port Townsend—dropped to the floor with a loud crash. I jerked backward as it exploded into a hundred fragments all over the kitchen.

"God!" I said. "What's wrong with me?"

My hands had flown to each side of my face at the sound of the breaking plate, and now I was rubbing my temples.

"It's okay. It's only a plate," Chuck said.

"It just surprised me. That bang."

"It's all right. You're tired," he said. "Where's your broom?"

"I'll clean it."

"Just get the broom."

I fetched the broom and the dustpan from the hallway closet and then watched as Chuck swept all of the scattered pieces of the plate into a pile, swept the pile into the dustpan, and dumped all of the pieces into the plastic garbage bin under my sink.

"You going to be okay?" he asked me.

"Yeah," I said.

He looked at me a moment, and then he put a hand on each of my shoulders and his eyes were on mine, and I knew right then he was going to kiss me, because otherwise what was he doing here, in my apartment, washing my dishes and sweeping up my mess? God, I wanted him to kiss me. In my head I was already kissing him back, and my hands were in his hair, and I was smelling that soapy smell of his. And right then, just as I began to lean into him, Chuck's hands suddenly fell away. He looked at me—stared at me, really—and for the life of me, I had no idea what was going on.

"I think I better take off," is all he said.

And before I could think of a response, he'd walked out my door.

# 21

Tuesday night, Lisa took me to a terrible bar downtown, a real singles joint, bright and immaculate and filled with desperate-looking women and even more desperate-looking men. There was a lot of laughter bouncing around from all corners, fake, loud laughter proving to anyone within earshot that a good time was being had by all. And there I was, with all of the other desperadoes. Forget baldness, belly fat, or bad breath. Desperation is the single most unattractive quality in the universe.

"You're kidding, right?" I said to Lisa after we'd found a couple of empty stools at the bar.

"Give it five minutes," she said. "You'll see."

"God, I can't hear a thing with so many biological clocks ticking in here."

"You know, you might meet someone nice."

"Oh, right. I forgot the plan. Come to a singles bar, meet a nice guy."

Lisa looked at me and sighed. "You are *so* out of practice," she said. "Look what you're wearing."

"What's wrong with this?"

"Well, at least unbutton it a little bit."

"Who are you?"

"I'm not kidding. It says 'frigid' right on your forehead."

"It says 'Get the fuck away from me' right on my forehead."

"Do you want to meet a guy or not?"

"No. I told you that. I do not want to meet a guy. This is all your idea."

"Ten o'clock. Take a look."

I turned my head to look in the ten o'clock position: man with longish hair and leather car coat, drinking a Budweiser from the bottle.

"He's cute," Lisa said.

"Okay, so he's not bad. From a distance, anyway."

"I'll be right back," she said.

Lisa got up, strode directly to the man in the leather car coat, and said something in his ear. A moment later, the man stood and accompanied her back to our stools.

"Rena, Timothy. Timothy, Rena."

Timothy held out his hand to shake mine. He had a weak handshake.

"Nice to meet you, Rena," he said.

"Hi," I said.

"Mind if I join you?"

I made a face that I hoped expressed my utter ambivalence, and Timothy took that for an invitation. While he went to retrieve a stool from farther down the bar, I asked Lisa what she'd said to him.

"I said you'd just had a death in the family and you were feeling a bit down, and maybe he wanted to come over and help me cheer you up."

"Wow. Thanks a lot."

Timothy returned with the stool and shoved it close to the two of us.

"You girls need a beer?" he asked.

"I don't know," I said. "Do we girls need a beer?"

"Yes," Lisa said. She gave me a hard look.

"Okay, then," Timothy said. He waved at the bartender. "Three more," he said, waving his Budweiser bottle in front of his face. He looked at me. "Bud okay?"

"Whatever," I said.

"I'll be right back," Lisa said.

"Where are you going?" I asked.

"Ladies'."

She took off, leaving me alone with Timothy. He smiled at me with closed lips. I could tell he had no idea what to say. Up close, his leather jacket looked like pleather. And his longish hair had been seriously groomed to give the appearance of being tossed back casually from his forehead. I could sense him sizing me up: Fuckable? Not fuckable?

"So, Rena," he said. "What do you do?"

"Me? Oh. Not much."

He laughed, like I'd said something funny.

"No, actually, I work with Lisa. At a restaurant."

"Ah," he said.

"We're wait*persons*."

"Oh. Where?" he asked.

"Sammy's Place?"

He nodded. His eyes darted around the room.

"How about you?" I asked.

"I'm in construction."

The bartender brought us our beers, and I took a swig from my bottle. I don't drink beer, so it tasted terrible.

"Houses?" I asked to be nice.

"Houses, hotels, office buildings, you name it."

I nodded. This conversation was going nowhere. From behind us came the sound of women laughing and then one loud hoot, like a bird screeching.

"So, you had a relative die, I hear," he said.

I nodded. Then I shook my head. "Yeah. Well. Not exactly."

"Not exactly?"

"No. Lisa pretty much made that one up."

"Oh."

"Sorry."

"I've heard worse."

"Well, the super of my building. He died. Does that count?"

Timothy didn't know what to say.

"I guess not," I said.

Timothy nodded.

"He was old," I said.

"I see."

"Died of old age."

"Uh-huh."

"Eighty-eight years old."

"Oh. Eighty-eight. That is old."

"Yeah. It is."

He shook his head as though he were thinking about it. We had just about covered everything we could think of, so it was a good thing Lisa came back right then. She settled down on her stool and took a sip from her bottle of beer.

"I miss anything?" she said.

"Will you girls excuse me a minute? I see someone I need to talk to," Timothy said.

He picked up his beer and wandered toward the back of the bar.

"What did you say to him?"

"I didn't say anything."

"God, and he was cute, too."

"You know, I don't think this is going to work."

"You haven't even tried."

"I think it has to be more, I don't know, organic. I don't think I can meet a guy in a bar."

"Organic?"

"You know. Like it just happens."

"Nothing just happens. You have to make things happen."

"Well, that's the thing. First you have to know what you

want. Then, you make it happen. I'm sort of stuck on part one."

Lisa shrugged.

"I think there's something wrong with me, anyway," I said.

"There are many things wrong with you. Which one are we talking about?"

"Chuck didn't even try to kiss me. Not once."

"Maybe he's shy."

"Maybe there's something wrong with me."

"Yeah. There is. You're all fucked up."

"You mind if we go?" I asked.

"You're giving up here?"

"I'm giving up here."

"Okay," she said. "But never say I didn't try."

"I will never say that."

The problem with Seattle is that there's nowhere to go at night. It's not like some cities, where the streets continue to bustle with activity well into the late hours and often into the dawn. Seattle is an indoor kind of place, big on reading and knitting and high in suicide statistics—probably from all of the lonely reading and solitary knitting going on behind closed doors. Which is to say that even though I didn't want to go upstairs to my apartment after Lisa dropped me off, I didn't have anywhere else to go. Standing in the alcove of my building, I had one of those moments of paralysis when a decision needs to be made by a person utterly unequipped to make a decision. Go upstairs? Go out? Go upstairs? Go out? My mind bounced back and forth between those two polar opposites until I couldn't stand it any longer. I got in my car and drove.

I didn't have any particular destination in mind, so don't think that I knew from the get-go that I'd be headed over to Brian's. Certainly, some part of my subconscious must have known that the place where I'd end up would be the one place I had told myself I wouldn't go.

I parked in front of his house, got out of my car, and stood there for a moment. I didn't have any particular plan in mind. I walked into Brian's backyard and looked into a window that turned out to be the kitchen. No one there. I kept walking, peering into windows, and seeing nothing but darkness. When I got to the front of the house, I climbed the porch stairs and leaned to the right, over the railing, to see inside the living room. There were Brian and Derrick, drinking beers, Brian leaning back in a truly gaudy black leather recliner and Derrick on a couch I recognized as the one that used to sit in Brian's apartment before he moved in with Anna. On the back wall hung a large framed Ansel Adams photograph of a tree.

I knocked on the door, and a minute later, Brian squinted through the door's tiny pane of glass.

"It's me," I said.

He opened the door.

"Hey," he said. "It's you."

His voice came out creaky, like he was out of practice. He smiled at me, a sort of stupid smile, the kind that let me know he'd had no idea I would be stopping by.

"Come in. Come in," he said.

He stood back to let me pass, and I walked into the living room to find Derrick rising from his seat.

"Hey, Derrick," I said.

Derrick looked at me, and his eyes went wide. His face blushed red all the way to his earlobes. I wondered what they'd been talking about before I showed up.

"I was just taking off," Derrick said.

"You don't have to go," I said.

"Yes, he does," Brian said.

Derrick grabbed his jacket from the sofa and threw his arms in the sleeves.

"Tomorrow, Bri," he said.

"Stay," I said.

"No, really. I'm not kidding. I was just leaving," Derrick said. He looked at Brian.

"Okay, then, buddy," Brian said. "Talk to you later."

"Right," Derrick said. "Nice to see you, Rena."

And with that, he walked out the front door. Brian shut the door behind him, turned around, and looked at me. He looked a little bit crazy right then. Crazy with relief.

"He didn't have to leave," I said.

"Oh, man, am I happy to see you," he said.

"Well, I really don't know what I'm doing here."

"God, this is great."

"No. Really. I shouldn't have come."

"Yes. You should have. God. You look great. You look beautiful. You do. God, have I missed you."

He put a hand on each of my arms and looked at my face as though I'd been the one who'd been missing for weeks on end and not him. Then he pulled me to his chest and wrapped his arms around me.

"Oh, man," he said.

"I hate you," I said.

"Yeah."

"I do."

"I know."

"You don't know. I really, really hate you."

"Yeah. Shhhhh."

"Don't shhhhh me."

"Shhhhh."

"I hate you."

Brian pulled away and looked at me.

"Hey, I have a present for you," he said.

"Yeah, I can imagine."

"No. Really. Come here."

He took me by the hand and walked me down the dark hallway of the house. I could hear the echo our footsteps made on the wood floor. For a house where two people lived together, it seemed awfully empty of possessions.

"I still hate you, even if you really did get me a present," I said.

"I know."

He pulled me into a bedroom—his bedroom, the one he shared with Anna, and sat me on the bed in the darkness.

"I don't like this," I said.

Brian let go of my hand and opened the drawer of a dresser.

"Here," he said. "I actually bought you this in Colorado. You know. When I left on that trip."

"Oh, yeah. *That* trip."

He handed me something wrapped in white tissue paper, and for just a moment I thought it was going to be an engagement ring, the one he was supposed to have given me months before. But the package was far too big to be an engagement ring, and when I unwrapped it I saw in the half light that it was a carved wooden bird painted black with yellowish streaks on the wings. I didn't know what to say. Had I asked for a carved black bird? I didn't think so. But it was just like Brian to give me something I would never want. One time, he'd actually brought me back the severed leg of an owl he'd hacked off himself from an owl corpse he'd found in the road. Look, it's not like I have to have jewelry or perfume, but I think the severed leg of an owl is going a bit too far for anyone's idea of a decent gift.

"Thanks," I said.

"Come here."

"I'm already here."

He kissed me then, and I let him. Why did he give me a bird?

"What?" he said to me.

He kissed me again, and I wondered why it was that all of it seemed to be happening to someone else and not me.

And I told myself to stop thinking.

I told myself, Rena, he's back. Brian is back and he still loves you and you still love him and here he is, the love of your life, taking off your clothes, and pulling you down onto his bed, and doing all of those sweet familiar moves you remember him doing for seven long years, so, girl, stop thinking so much and just be happy, be happy, be happy.

# 22

I was just on the verge of waking up the next morning—still a foot or so beneath the surface of consciousness—when someone knocked on my apartment door, pulling me up from the dream world. I looked at the clock. Noon. I'd come home in the middle of the night, climbed into bed, and completely conked out. I must have locked the door behind me when I got home.

"Who is it?" I yelled.

"Alicia!"

"Just a second!"

I pulled my arms into an old cardigan that I realized in that moment actually belonged to Alicia and opened the door.

"Like your sweater," she said.

"Good morning," I said.

"Can I come in?"

"Sure."

"Don't put on any pants on my account."

"What's going on? No, give me one second. I'm freezing."

I scavenged through my closet until I came up with an old pair of sweatpants and pulled them on. When I came out again, Alicia was sitting on my sofa, kneading her hands together.

"Okay. So. What's going on?" I asked.

I took a seat next to her on the sofa and studied her head. She wasn't wearing a wig, and she wasn't wearing a scarf. No, it was her own hair I was looking at, curly and black and with the bangs held back by a small brown barrette. She looked adorable.

"Alicia?" I said.

My sister's eyes filled with tears.

"Sorry," she said. "Just give me a minute."

"That's okay," I said. "Want some tissue?"

She reached into a pocket of her coat and pulled out a package of Kleenex, which she held up to show me.

"I came prepared," she said.

She plucked one of the tissues from the package and blew her nose into it.

"I'm sorry," she said again.

"Quit saying that."

"It's Aryeh," she said.

I nodded and looked at her encouragingly, but she didn't say anything more.

"What about Aryeh?" I said.

"We had a fight."

"About your hair?"

"Yes. No. Well, the hair started it. And then it just sort of took off from there. And he just yelled at me. I mean, yelled. And I guess I yelled back. Anyway, there was a lot of yelling. And pretty soon I couldn't take it anymore and I just left."

She cried into the damp tissue, crumpled it into a ball, and used the crumpled ball to wipe her face.

"What was he yelling?"

Alicia dropped the tissue onto my floor.

"Oh, you know. How I couldn't take off the wig now, not after this amount of time, and what about the kids, they'll be so confused, and how I owed it to them, and how I owed it to him, and you know what I said? I said I don't owe you anything."

"Uh-huh."

"And then I told him if he thought I owed him something, then maybe we weren't going to agree on anything, because that is the most basic thing, isn't it? That we're equal and that we don't owe each other? God, I hate that he said that to me. I don't owe anybody anything!"

She pulled another tissue free and blew her nose again. She shook her head.

"I don't know, Rena," she said. "I don't even know if he loves me."

"He loves you. Of course he loves you."

"I don't know."

"Every couple has fights."

Alicia's chest heaved up and down as she took a few shaky breaths. "Not like this."

"Yes. Like this. Come on."

"I don't know what I'm going to do."

I didn't know either. But I wasn't going to say that to her. "Look," I said. "Later today, when things are calmer, you guys can talk again."

Alicia looked out the window toward the sky. "Yeah," she said. "Probably."

She seemed to be done talking for the moment, so I took that as a hint that I should stop talking, too. I thought about this one time when I'd visited Alicia at home—this would have been months and months ago—and for some reason we both decided it would be a hoot for me to try on her wigs. So we took all of her wigs into the bathroom, locked the door, and one by one pulled them onto my head while we screamed with laughter. I don't know why it was so funny to see me wear a wig when it wasn't at all funny to see Alicia wearing one, but it just was. Alicia decided the light brown bob with the straight-across bangs looked the best, so she had me put that one on, and then she gave me a few coats of plum-colored lipstick, and after that she painted my eyelids with black liner, and then she decided I needed mascara, too, and by the time she was done fixing me up, I looked like a drag queen. It was horrifying.

My cell phone rang, and I grabbed for it off the coffee table. The screen said "Aryeh."

"It's him," I said.

"I don't want to talk to him."

I pressed the "talk" button.

"She doesn't want to talk to you."

"Put her on, Rena."

I turned to Alicia. "He says to put you on."

"I don't want to talk to him."

"She doesn't want to talk to you."

"Hand her the phone."

I handed my sister the phone.

"Go on," I said. "Talk to him."

Alicia glared at me, but she took the phone out of my hand.

"What?" she said into the phone.

I whispered, "I'll just wait in the bathroom."

"How can you say that?" my sister was saying to her husband as I shut the bathroom door.

I turned on the fan so that I wouldn't hear anything, brushed my teeth, and tried to do something to tame my hair. Pretty soon I'd played with it too much—always a mistake with curly hair—and my only remaining option was to tie it all into a ponytail at the back of my head, a style that makes me look about twelve. I put an ear against the door to hear if Alicia was done and heard the murmur of her voice. Still talking. I hoped they were working something out.

There was no use looking for something else to do to keep my mind off of the night before, so I sat down on the closed toilet seat, bit at my fingernails, and played over the whole thing in my head. I had no idea where the two of us stood, or what the night before had meant, or even if it meant anything at all. And the fact that I didn't know made me angry—not at Brian, but at myself. What was I doing?

And then it occurred to me that he hadn't even called me yet, and here it was, past noon already.

I put my ear to the bathroom door again, and this time I heard two voices, and for a moment I thought maybe Aryeh had been calling from the front of my building and had now leapt up the stairs to retrieve his wife. But no, the voice wasn't low enough to be Aryeh. Maybe it was Brian? I wasn't ready to see him again so soon. I turned off the fan, cracked open the door, and nearly hit Alicia with it.

"Oh!" she said. "I was just coming to get you. Chaim's here."

"Chuck?"

I stepped out of the bathroom and there stood Chuck, looking like he'd just gotten out of bed and that he'd slept in the clothes he was wearing. He didn't look very chipper. In fact, he looked fairly wiped out. He had a blue watch cap on his head, with the brim pulled down to his eyes, and a huge ribbed sweater, frayed all around the hem.

"You okay?" I asked him.

He pointed, and when I looked in the direction where he was pointing, there lay the Big Guy, half-asleep on my sofa, his big tongue hanging out of his big mouth, as though he'd never gone anywhere.

"Oh, my God!" I said.

"He was at Green Lake," Chuck said. "I was just riding

by—this was last night—and I thought I saw a dog that looked like him, so I rode around looking until I found him and then you weren't around so I took him home and now, well, here he is."

"You!" I said to the Big Guy.

I petted his back and stuck my face into the fur of his back. He smelled terrible.

"Where have you been, you little turkey?" I said to him. "We were so worried about you! Are you hungry? I bet you're hungry. You want some food, Big Guy? Some water?"

I looked at Chuck. I'd never met someone like him before—someone who did so much for everybody else: coming to Shabbat at Alicia's, going out to dinner with my mom and Ron, trying to help me return the dog, coming to the hospital with me to bring Carl his things, and now this. Finding the Big Guy. What kind of dumb luck had brought Chuck into my life?

"God! Thank you so much! I can't believe you found him!"

"Maybe I should go?" Alicia said.

I'd forgotten all about my sister.

"Oh! No, you don't have to go. Stay. I want to hear what Aryeh said and everything."

"I should be the one to go," Chuck said.

"No, no, no," my sister said. "Really. I'm going home now and you two just stay right here and I'm so glad Chaim found your dog, Rena. Really. And I'll call you later."

"Nobody go!" I said.

At the sound of my loud voice, the Big Guy raised his head and looked at me.

"You're in big trouble, young man," I said to him.

"Yeah, so, I came by last night after I found him," Chuck said. "I borrowed my friend's car. It was probably, I don't know, ten-thirty, something like that. And you weren't here, so I waited outside of your door."

"Oh," I said. "Yeah. I was out. With Lisa."

Chuck nodded. "Right. Well, anyway. I waited until about two."

"Two? You waited that long?"

"Yeah."

I nodded.

"And then, I don't know, on the way back to my apartment, I got this idea to swing by your old boyfriend's house, because it seemed to me that maybe I could just put the dog back, you know, the way we'd planned it when he ran away."

I felt something in my stomach twist.

"And it was funny," Chuck said, "because your car was parked there."

I didn't say anything. What could I say?

"So. Anyway," Chuck said. "I'm going to take off now. And I guess you can return the dog yourself."

He turned and walked toward my apartment door.

"Chuck," I said.

"No, no. It's okay," he said.

He stopped at the doorway and looked back for a moment. "Best of luck, Rena," he said, before leaving.

I could feel Alicia's eyes on me.

"Not one word," I said to her.

Alicia put both hands in the air, the way you'd do if you were being arrested.

"I'm not saying anything," she said.

"Because I'm not talking about it."

"That's fine. Don't have to talk about it."

"I don't want to hear what an idiot I am."

"Nobody's calling you an idiot."

"I am. I'm a total fucking idiot."

"Yeah," my sister said. "You are."

# 23

Brian's front door was unlocked when I got there, so I walked in, the Big Guy on his leash beside me.

"Brian?" I called out. "You home?"

Nobody answered.

"Brian?" I yelled again.

Somewhere a shower was running. I walked down the hallway to the bedroom and found the bathroom door left open to let out the steam. From behind the shower curtain came the plunking sound of a bar of soap dropping.

"Lay down," I said to the Big Guy.

Brian's bed was still a jumble of sheets and blankets from the night before, and I took a moment to sort of straighten everything out before I sat down. In the daylight, I could plainly see Anna's fleecy things hanging in the closet, her climbing shoes on the closet floor. Everything she wore looked exactly like Brian's except smaller. I could barely breathe. This was

Anna's room, Anna's space. Brian had fucked us both, literally and figuratively.

The shower stopped, and I pictured Brian drying himself off and then wiping the mist from the mirror to shave. A drawer opened and closed. Brian was humming something I didn't recognize. Then the fan switched off.

"Brian?" I said.

"God!" he said before he saw me.

"Sorry. Your door was unlocked."

Brian wasn't wearing anything, and he made no effort to reach for his clothes.

"No. I'm glad you're here," he said. "You just startled me."

"I brought your dog back."

"What?"

"Your dog."

"Oh!" he said, seeing the Big Guy lying on the floor. "God! You found him?"

"No."

"Hiya, Tilly," he said. "Come here, boy."

The Big Guy made no effort to move.

"I took him," I said.

"What do you mean, you took him?"

"I mean, I took him in the first place, and now I'm bringing him back."

"You, what?" Brian said. "You're shitting me."

I shook my head.

"You took him? Oh, my God. Why would you do that?"

A smile was beginning to creep across his face.

"Look," I said. "I came over to bring him back and apologize. So. I'm sorry I took Anna's dog."

Brian threw back his head and laughed. "Oh, God, you are just adorably nutso, you know that?"

"No. I'm not."

"Yes, you are. God. What were you thinking?"

"I don't know," I said.

"You are too funny," he said.

He put a hand on my head and mussed my hair, as if I were a little kid.

"Stop it," I said.

With both hands, Brian pressed me down on the bed until I was lying flat on my back with my feet still on the floor. Then he lay down next to me, on his side, and put an arm across my body.

"I can't be with you," I said.

Brian kissed my ear. "Shhh," he said.

"Brian, it's over. For real."

"Stop talking, my little criminal. My little jealous criminal."

I pushed his arm off me and sat up.

"Tell me something," I said. "When do you plan on calling Anna to tell her you're breaking up with her?"

Brian lifted himself up to lean back on the bed on both elbows. "I have to go to Montana," he said.

"What do you mean, you have to go to Montana?"

"Her parents are expecting to meet me."

"So, you're going to Montana to meet her parents before you break up with her?"

"You know, it's complicated."

"Yeah. It is. It's really complicated."

"Come on, Rena. We're always going to be us. Brian and Rena. Forever. No matter who we're with, you know?"

"Is that what you think?"

"You know that. We're always going to love each other."

I shook my head. I didn't have any more time to waste on Brian Benning. I'd been stuck in a time warp the last few months, waiting for Brian to decide he wanted me back, and in the meantime I'd been so absorbed in the drama of it all that I'd lost track of the people I cared about. I didn't want to be that person anymore. I wanted to be a better person. I stood up, and the Big Guy raised his head to look at me.

"I've got to go," I said to my old boyfriend.

"No, you don't."

"Yes, I really do."

I stood up.

"Brian," I said, "I hope you're very happy. I mean that."

I looked at the Big Guy.

"Good-bye, sweetie," I said.

On Sunday, I went to Carl's funeral. The service was listed in the newspaper, not a full obituary but a short notice that gave the time and the place—the chapel on the grounds of a cemetery in north Seattle—and it seemed only proper that I should go and pay my last respects. How many people were going to show up for an old guy like Carl, anyway? I wanted there to be someone in attendance for him besides a handful of relatives and a chaplain who probably didn't know Carl from Adam.

It was a cold day, the sky its usual color of wet cement. Maybe it would rain later, maybe not—I'd brought along an umbrella just in case. When I pulled up outside of the chapel, I had no trouble finding a parking space. The lot was nearly empty.

Inside, a stick of a man in a dark suit, with thin strands of gray hair swept back from his forehead, handed me a program and then directed me to take a seat in one of the pews on the left. In the pews on the right, I recognized Carl's son sitting with a woman—his wife?—and a couple of younger men. That was it. Five of us. In the very front lay Carl inside of an open coffin. I could see only the side of his face, which shined with a waxy glow. Next to the coffin was a small table with a few framed photographs set on top that I supposed were for guests to take a look at. From where I sat, I could see that one of the photos showed Carl in his military uniform—the navy, I think. If I'd ever listened to his stories in the alcove, maybe I'd know what division of the military he'd served in. Also what war.

"Are we ready?" the man with the thin strands of hair asked Carl's son.

Carl's son looked around the room, saw me, and smiled

with recognition. Then he nodded at the man with the thinning hair.

"Let us begin," the man said loudly, as though the room were filled with mourners and he wanted to be certain he could be heard by the people in the back.

I didn't listen. I sat and waited and tried not to think about the fact that Carl was dead and only a few feet away from me. Jews don't have open-casket funerals, and the whole thing was too foreign and creepy for me. But there really was nowhere else to look, so I found myself looking at Carl and thinking about dead him, and soon enough, I was crying.

When Carl's son stood up in front of the room to talk about his dad for a few minutes, I took the opportunity to scrounge through my handbag in search of a tissue. I couldn't believe I had forgotten to bring one along. Chances had been excellent that I was going to cry—I always cry at funerals because they are always sad, no matter how good a life the person led or how nontragic their ending. In fact, I always cry at just about any old event—births, bar mitzvahs, weddings, you name it. But no. No tissue. Not even an old, used, scrunched-up one. I reached up and wiped at my face with the side of my hand. It occurred to me that I could have used the hem of my blouse for a hanky and no one would have noticed, but I didn't want to be rude.

Brian had called me twice over the last few days and left a couple of text messages, but I never picked up when I saw it was him, and I never called back. The truth was, I didn't have anything else to say to him. It was Chuck I wanted to hear from, and Chuck who never called. I didn't blame him. Why would he want to waste his time on someone as messed up as me? He deserved so much better.

Carl's son was talking about Carl's method for teaching his son to drive, which had been pretty much handing his son the car keys and wishing him luck.

"That was my dad in a nutshell," Carl's son said. "He had faith you could do things yourself."

My nose was dripping. I sniffled as quietly as I could, not wanting Carl's family to think a crazy woman had shown up at his funeral. They were all dry-eyed as could be. I was giving my handbag one more search for something to wipe my nose with when suddenly a hand appeared at the side of my head, holding a tissue. I turned. Chuck.

"Hey," he whispered.

"Hey," I whispered back. "Thanks."

"You okay?" he asked me.

"Yeah."

He came around the side of the pew to sit in my row, and I shoved over to make room for him. I knew he hadn't come for me—he'd come for Carl—but still, I was happy to see him.

"Here. Take all of them," he whispered, handing me a few more tissues. "They've got a box of them by the door."

There was a loud *thunk* and I realized that Carl's son and the chaplain had closed the casket. It seemed the service was over. Apparently, we weren't all going to go stand by the grave and put dirt on the coffin like you do at a Jewish funeral. We were leaving Carl where he was and they'd bury him later. I stood and then checked the floor to make sure I hadn't left any used tissues behind, and when I looked up, there was Carl's son waiting to shake my hand and thank me for coming.

"Very nice of you," he said.

"No," I said. "Not really. I wanted to come."

"Well, thank you anyway," he said. "I'd invite you to our house for tea, but we're not going back to the house just yet."

"Oh, no," I said. "I have to be going anyway."

"And you are?" he said, holding out a hand to Chuck.

"Oh, I'm sorry," I said. "This is my friend Chuck. He came to the hospital that night. When your dad went there."

"Good to meet you, Chuck. Nice of you to come with Rena."

"I'm sorry for your loss," Chuck said.

Carl's son strolled back down the aisle to meet up with his family, and the two of us walked out of the funeral chapel to find a light drizzle falling from overhead even though the skies had cleared.

"Thanks for coming," I said.

Chuck shrugged.

"I miss Carl," I said. "I really do."

"I could start talking about some archaic subject out of the blue, if you'd like."

"No, thanks."

We walked toward the parking lot. My car was the only one there.

"How'd you get here?" I asked.

"Bus."

I smiled. "Can I give you a ride home?"

Chuck shook his head. "Nah," he said. "I think I'll walk."

"Okay."

"So. Brian pretty surprised to get his dog back?"

"I guess so. Yeah. He was. He's gone now. To Montana. To meet the girlfriend's parents."

Chuck nodded.

"Let me give you a ride, would you?" I said.

"No. Really. I feel like walking. I do."

"Okay."

There was nothing more to do but get into my car, turn on the engine, and watch Chuck grow smaller and smaller in my rearview mirror until, finally, I couldn't see him anymore.

# 24

My mother and Ron got married six months later. They had a small ceremony in my mother's backyard, under a chuppah that Ron had crocheted himself. A woman rabbi conducted the service, which didn't please Aryeh, but he was a sport about the whole thing and showed up despite the heresy. It seemed he and Alicia were working things out. My sister—who still hadn't gone back to wearing a wig—had happily compromised for the occasion by wearing a hat. No one told their kids to stop running around, so there were a few moments when you couldn't hear what was being said, but at a wedding we all know what's being said anyway. Love. Vows. Promises. Forever.

Al was there with Melanie, and they looked very sweet together. She'd turned out to be a fairly attractive middle-aged woman. Sort of earthy and hippieish, with long brown hair and fat calves. The two of them held hands during the ceremony like a pair of high schoolers.

And Chuck was there, too, filming. I hadn't seen him since Carl's funeral, and I kept stealing glances at him while trying not to be too obvious about it. He looked the same as ever—wrinkled shirt, messy hair, baggy pants—except that he'd added a blazer to the mix. And he was clean shaven. He had a small dimple in his chin that I hadn't known about.

After the ceremony, while the guests milled about, drinking champagne and snacking on the weird little sandwiches my mother had ordered from a kosher kitchen, I finally got up the nerve to approach him.

"Hey," I said. "You shaved."

He smiled, then leaned forward to give me a friendly kiss on the cheek.

"Nice to see you," he said. He reached up to touch his chin. "Yeah, I'm beginning to regret it. Too much upkeep."

"It's good on you," I said. "I like it."

"Thanks."

We stood for a moment, looking at each other.

"So, what's going on with you?" he asked. "I stopped by the restaurant once to see you a while ago, but you'd already quit."

"You did?"

"Yeah. So, good for you."

"Yeah. Good for me."

"You get another job?"

"I'm working for my dad. He's thrilled. Always wanted a son to take over the business, you know. Who knew there'd be so much to learn about toilets?"

"Fascinating stuff. Toilets," he said.

"Until you really think about them."

"I try to avoid really thinking about toilets."

"Yeah. Well, I don't have that luxury anymore."

He smiled, and the little dimple in his chin disappeared.

"I'm pretty much done with the filming," he said. "You want to sit down?"

We wandered over to the dessert table and filled a plate with cookies. Then we found a table in the far corner of the yard. My mother had been lucky to get a sunny day for her wedding. Nothing in her garden had been in bloom, so she'd bought a number of potted plants and set them around here and there for color. I was sure to be killing one of those potted plants in the very near future, as my mother had already told me to be sure and take one home after the reception.

"You want to hear something funny?" I asked.

"Sure."

"I'm actually good at it. At designing bathrooms, I mean. That's what I do mostly. People come in and I help them decide what would look good in their house."

"I'm sure that's true. I mean, you could tell just by looking at your apartment that you're a good designer."

"Oh, come on! My apartment was a mess when you saw it."

"I still could tell. You had a certain . . . style. People are very lucky to have you design their bathrooms."

"Stop."

"I'm not joking!"

"Okay, you're not joking," I said. "So. Then. Thanks."

"You're welcome."

"I'm taking a course in interior design. It's just a beginner thing, over in Bellevue. But I'm enjoying it."

"God, that's great."

"So, what about you?" I asked. "What have you been up to?"

He shrugged. "I've had a lot of work lately. Spring's a busy time for weddings. Not too much time for my own stuff at the moment. But it'll come."

I looked around the yard and tried to think of something else to say. Chuck studied the cookie plate and finally picked up a chocolate macaroon.

"So," he said. "Brian still . . . where did he go? Montana?"

"I don't know. I think so. We don't really talk anymore. I mean, we don't talk anymore at all."

I chose a toffee bar off the plate, even though I had no intentions of eating it. Somewhere in the distance, my mother was calling out to everyone that it was time to catch the bouquet.

"So, why did you stop by?" I asked.

"Excuse me?"

"You said you dropped by the restaurant. Just wanted to . . . say hello?"

"Yeah," he said. "Say hello. See how you were doing."

"That was nice of you."

He shrugged. I couldn't stop myself.

"So. You seeing anybody?" I asked.

"No," he said. "I'm not. You?"

I shook my head.

"Rena!" my mother yelled. "Come catch it!"

"Just a second!" I yelled back. I looked at Chuck. "I have to go," I said.

Chuck reached up and ran a finger along the slope of my nose.

"You better go," he said.

Neither one of us moved.

"Rena!" my mother yelled.

"Hey," Chuck said. "Did you ever get around to watching *Citizen Kane*?"

I shook my head.

"You *still* haven't seen it?"

I shook my head.

"What am I going to do with you?"

I shrugged.

"Rena! Get over here!"

Now my dad was yelling.

"Your mother needs you!" he called out.

"Your mother needs you," Chuck said to me.

I smiled at him. "So, maybe you want to watch it with me?" I asked.

"I'd like that."

"Rena, for crying out loud!" my dad yelled.

"Okay," I said. "When?"

"Tonight?" Chuck said.

"I'm throwing it!" my mother yelled.

Do you remember when I said that a person never knows what the future might bring? Well, right about then, I was pretty sure I knew.

"On my way!" I yelled back.

## ACKNOWLEDGMENTS

Thank you to everybody I've ever known.

In particular, thank you: Janet Dorfman, Sarah Burnes, Hilary Rubin Teeman, Sharon Strauss, Dinah Manoff, Eric Lidji, Jonathan Evison, Nancy Blakey, Marilynn Gottlieb, Chana Gudelsky, Robin Simons, Dr. Shirley Guterson, Murray Guterson, my fellow Friday Victrolians, and all the good people at Eagle Harbor Books.

Thank you to my biggest fans and favorite people: Hannah and Gillon Crichton.

I am forever indebted to my mother-in-law, the late, great Judy Crichton, for her generosity, love, and unconditional support.

And finally, it's impossible to thank Rob Crichton enough—for everything.